SPACESHIP
OVER NORTH DAKOTA

Another book
by KEVIN KREMER:

A Kremer Christmas Miracle

Spaceship
Over North Dakota

by Kevin Kremer

Illustrated by Dave Ely

Published by Sweetgrass Communications
1996
P.O. Box 3221
Bismarck, ND 58502

ISBN 0-9632837-4-X

Printed in the U.S.A.
1996

*This book is dedicated to my AMAZING former students! Many of them are characters in this book. Thanks for teaching me so much more than I could **ever** teach you!*

SPECIAL THANKS FROM THE AUTHOR...

- To George Keiser, Erik Sakariassen, and Paul Sakariassen for making the publishing of this book possible!

- To Dave Ely, a former student of mine, for illustrating the book!

- To Matthew Fettig for being a great inspiration to me!

- To Janelle Michelsen for her tremendous enthusiasm!

- To everyone who encouraged me to write a second book!

- To the fifth graders from Carl Ben Eielson School in Grand Forks for all their help!

- To Pam Passariello and her students from McKenzie School for their kindness and support!

- To the Kremer Family for their constant support!

- To the following teachers and their students for providing suggestions for improving this book:

Sue Triska	Evelyn Spangler
Darlene Paulson	Kim Knutson
Alice Carufel	Sharlene Gusaas
Melanie Crawford	Karol Volk
Merilynn Starck	Duane Roth

CHAPTER I

It was late in the fourth quarter at the Fiesta Bowl! Only five seconds remained on the clock! Our team, the Nebraska Cornhuskers, trailed the Florida Gators by five points–33-28. We had the ball. There was only enough time left for one pass play into the end zone. As quarterback of Nebraska, I knew it was up to me and my favorite receiver, Chad Renner, to win the National Championship for our team!

(Actually, my good friend, Chad, and I were down in my basement in our family room, with a red Nerf football, acting out our fantasy of playing for The University of Nebraska in the National Championship Game.)

The ball was hiked to me, and I dropped back, looking for Chad to get free in the end zone so I could throw him the football. (In fact, Chad hiked the ball to me at one end of our family room and then ran toward the sofa at the other end of the room.)

Two defenders shadowed Chad closely as he

approached the end zone, while three huge Gator linemen were ready to sack me and end the game in their favor. I had to release the ball, hoping intensely that Chad could somehow get to it, even while being closely covered by the two Gators. I threw the ball and was plastered to the ground! (Really, I threw the Nerf football and fell backwards onto our beanbag chair.)

I could only hope that Chad could somehow catch the ball! Chad leaped high into the air, caught the ball with an amazing fingertip catch, coming down with one foot in the end zone, scoring the winning touchdown! The crowd went absolutely bonkers! Nebraska won the National Championship!

(Actually, Chad *did* make a great leaping catch at the other end of the family room. Then he sprawled onto the sofa in triumph! Chad and I cheered enthusiastically!)

My mom interrupted our celebration as she called from the top of the stairs. "Chad and Kevin! The Governor's making that special announcement again!"

"What channel, Mom?" I yelled back.

"Channel 7," she answered.

"OK, Mom!" I hollered from the bottom of the stairs.

As Chad and I ran into my downstairs bedroom,

and I turned on my television, Chad said, "I saw this announcement yesterday. Sounds like the Governor wants every kid in every school in North Dakota watching television at ten o'clock tomorrow morning."

"I wonder why?" I responded.

"Who knows?" Chad replied. "He sure is getting everyone super-curious, though."

"No doubt," I nodded my agreement.

When we saw the Governor appear on the TV screen, Chad said, "Here he goes."

Chad and I plopped down on my bed, our heads facing the TV, to watch and listen. Governor Ed, apparently sitting behind the desk in his office at the Capitol in Bismarck, started speaking. "Hi, I'm Governor Ed," he began, with a smile on his face. "This announcement is for all students and teachers in North Dakota. Tomorrow, most of you will be attending your first day of classes for the new school year. At ten o'clock tomorrow morning, I will be bringing you an important and exciting message. All North Dakota television stations have agreed to carry my short speech at that time. I hope all of you will be watching. See you tomorrow."

At this point my mom came downstairs and joined Chad and me in my bedroom. She said, "I wonder what Governor Ed's going to be saying tomorrow. I don't ever remember any governor doing this before."

Chad said, "Whatever he has in mind, it will sure add some excitement to the first day of school."

"Speaking of the first day of school," my mom wondered, "are you two guys ready to start another year?"

Chad smiled slightly and said, "There's not much we can do about it, Mrs. Feeney. It's always a little hard giving up all the freedom of the summer, but at least Kevin and I got in the same room, and we got the teacher we both wanted."

"Ya, Mom," I agreed. "Dr. KK is probably the only person in the world that's crazier about sports than we are!"

"No doubt!" Chad added. "And we've got a bunch of our friends in our class this year, too."

"Any cute girls?" my mom inquired with a playful smile.

"Mom!" I said as if I were shocked with her question, but I really wasn't.

"Ya, Mrs. Feeney!" Chad insisted. "You know Kevin and I are too busy with sports to have time for *girls!*"

"Boys," Mom said, still smiling, "I have a feeling that's going to change before you know it."

CHAPTER II

My mom, Chad, and I were standing in my bedroom facing each other. "Mom?" I began. "A bunch of us want to get together at Prez's house at about four o'clock. Is that all right with you?" I asked hopefully.

"Just be back by six," Mom replied. "When your dad gets home from football practice, we're ordering pizza from A&B."

My dad is head football coach of the Bismarck High School Demons and also teaches physical education at Bismarck High.

"You know I wouldn't miss that," I assured my mom. "Do you think Chad can join us?"

"Would you like to have pizza with us, Chad?" my mom inquired.

Chad grinned and said, "Mrs. Feeney, there's no way I could pass up A&B pizza. I'll call and ask my mom when I'm at Prez's house."

My mom responded, "Sounds great, Chad."

Then, my mom inquired, "Did Prez get in your class this year?"

"Uh huh," I answered.

"Prez should help make this year interesting for you guys," Mom said.

My mom has been the physical education teacher at Dorothy Moses Elementary School, the same school that Chad and I attend, for many years. She taught Prez since kindergarten.

Mom keeps telling me that the group of kids that are sixth graders at Dorothy Moses this year, the group that Chad and Prez and I belong to, is the most amazing group that's gone through the school in all the years she's taught. Prez has *got* to be one of the main reasons for our class's reputation.

"How long has everyone been calling him Prez anyway?" Mom wondered.

Chad thought awhile and said, "I think we started calling him Prez in the second grade. I remember one day in Mrs. Carufel's class we all had to tell everyone what we wanted to be when we grew up. When it was Prez's turn, he said he wanted to be President of the United States. Shortly after that, it seemed like everyone was calling him Prez."

I added, "I'll bet a lot of people don't even remember his real name is Mike Gold. Even his parents call him Prez now."

Chad continued, "Prez still wants to be President, too. One thing's for sure. He definitely has the brains and the mouth to be President."

I chuckled a little and said, "He's probably *too* smart to be President."

"Good one, Kevin," my mom said with a giggle.

I looked at my Boston Celtics clock on the wall and said, "Chad, we'd better get going. It's almost four."

As the three of us walked upstairs, my mom said, "I'll see you guys later."

Chad and I walked through our kitchen and out the door that went into our garage. Once we were outside, we got on our bikes and headed for Prez's house a few blocks away.

Prez's house may be the messiest place on earth! Prez's parents are both college teachers, but you can tell that cleaning is not a priority for either of them.

Their large basement is where Prez spends most of his time. Both his parents encourage him to conduct any type of experiments and stuff down there as long as he doesn't start a fire or blow up anything! The basement looks like a mad scientist's laboratory–with computers, wires, test tubes, experiments, and indescribable gadgets all over the place!

When we got to Prez's house, we parked our bikes

on the driveway, went to the front door, and rang the doorbell. Soon, Prez's mother came to the door.

"Hi, boys," Prez's always-smiling mother said. She opened the front door and cordially suggested, "Go right on down. Some other boys are already down there."

When Chad and I got to the bottom of the stairs, our attention was instantly drawn toward a large object suspended from the ceiling near the middle of the basement. Prez was standing near it, along with Charles Riely, Jim Martinson, Nick Hillman, and Matt Bitz.

"What the heck!?" Chad exclaimed, his mouth wide open as we walked over to join our friends.

"Unreal!" I gasped, keeping my eyes on the large object as I got closer to it. Prez had constructed what looked like a large model of The Starship Exercise from the Star Track movies!

Prez looked at me with a proud smile, and said, "Just a little summer project I've been working on."

"I knew you were a big Star Track fan, but this is unbelievable!" Chad exclaimed.

"Does this thing fly?" I inquired.

"It should be ready for a test flight in a few weeks," Prez announced.

"You may have topped yourself!" I said with respect in my voice.

CHAPTER III

Prez smiled as he watched six of his good friends look over every inch of his creation. Prez even brought over some chairs for us to stand on so we could examine the part of the structure that hung above our heads. From what we could tell, Prez had captured almost every detail of the real Starship Exercise's construction.

With a sly grin on his face, Matt asked, "Prez, do you think you can get it to go as fast as the one in the movies?"

Prez looked at Matt, giggled a little, and said, "That might take me a year or two more."

"How long is this thing anyway?" Jim inquired as he stood on a chair looking everything over closely.

Prez answered as if he were in the Navy and was addressing his commanding officer, "Almost fifteen feet from stem to stern, sir!" Prez mimicked.

"How are you going to get this gigantic thing outside?" Nick asked.

Prez answered, "The Exercise can be separated into three pieces that just barely fit through our basement door. It comes apart *here* and *here*," he said, as he pointed to two locations near the center of the craft. "Then the craft can be reassembled in our garage and readied for flight."

"Where are you going to fly it?" Charles wondered.

Prez responded, "As long as the weather is reasonable, just about anywhere I want it to go."

"Do you mean anywhere, as in anywhere in *Bismarck?*" asked Chad.

"Actually, with the power and guidance systems on board, its range should be significantly beyond that," Prez replied.

Jim asked, "So, will you be able to fly it to Disneyland?"

With a totally serious look on his face, Prez answered, "Jim, you underestimate The Exercise."

I don't think any of us knew whether Prez was serious or not .

"How does it work?" I wondered, bracing myself for an explanation I probably wouldn't understand at all.

"Let's just say that The Starship Exercise combines the technologies of solar power, conventional propulsion systems, and the Goodyear Blimp," Prez replied. "I've used the information available from the GPS or Global Positioning Satellites so the Exercise should theoretically be able to fly anywhere it's programmed to go."

Prez walked over to a nearby table and picked up a device that looked a lot like the remote control unit for my radio controlled race car, only larger and more complex. Then, Prez continued, "When the Exercise isn't flying some pre-programmed flight pattern, I can use this remote control apparatus to maneuver the craft."

"You're unreal, Prez!" Charles exclaimed. "I hope you're going to let us help you with the test flights."

"That's what friends are for," Prez said, with a big smile.

"Guys," Prez began in a nearly-serious tone, "would you all promise to keep this project a secret until I give you the OK? I want to keep this venture as low key as possible until I'm ready for my first public flight."

"You can count on us, Prez," I said. I knew I spoke for everyone.

"Would you mind if I change the subject for awhile?" Prez inquired. Prez led us to another corner of his basement where there were two old large sofas, a beanbag chair, and a few other wooden chairs. The furniture was arranged in a semicircle facing a large screen.

"Make yourselves comfortable," Prez said as he walked to the front of the screen, facing us, where one of his computers was setting on a small table. He turned on his computer, pressed a few buttons, and a list soon appeared on the large screen in front of us.

Right away I recognized the list of names. It was the sixth grade class list for Dr. KK's class, the one that all of us would be in this year. After each name was a phone number.

Prez pointed toward the screen, and said, "I'm sure all of you recognize this as our class list for this year. I copied the list from the one that's been posted on the front door of the school since the second week in June."

"Hey!" Matt said excitedly. "I can't believe the great people we've got in our class this year!"

"Ya," Jim agreed wholeheartedly, "our class has brains, looks, and even superb athletic ability!"

"Which one of those qualities do you think *you* have?" I asked Jim in a teasing voice.

"Some of us have it *all*!" Jim announced in a joking manner.

That remark got a big laugh from all of us.

"Oh great!" Charles observed. "We've got Blaine Moze in our class this year!"

"That means we're going to have to get used to his rhyming all the time," Nick said. "I can't believe how he thinks of rhymes so quickly."

"It is pretty incredible," Chad said.

Then, noticing another name on the list, Chad stated, "Prez, it looks like Jan Pedersen's going to challenge you for the top grades again this year."

"I enjoy the competition she provides," Prez said confidently.

Nick saw Jacy Greff's name and said, "How about that Jacy? She's so nice, it's unreal."

"Ya," I agreed, "she's so nice, she makes Snow White look like a meany."

Everyone started laughing.

When the laughing stopped, Prez pointed at another name on the list and said, "I think all of us know everyone in our class this year except this guy, Mike Schaffer. Does anyone know anything about him?"

No one responded. Prez said, "No problem. We'll get to know him soon enough. I managed to get his phone number anyway."

I asked Prez, "What do you need all of the phone numbers for anyway?"

Prez answered, "I was just about to get to that." He paused for a brief moment and then continued, "I've got an idea for the first day of school that I wanted to share with you. It should help to start the year off on a positive note and help us get on the good side of Dr. KK."

Prez got a big smile on his face, and explained, "We all know that Dr. KK wears football jerseys almost every day to school. What if his whole class wore jerseys to school the very first day?!"

We looked around at each other with big smiles on our faces.

"He'd freak out!" Nick howled.

"Cool!" Charles added.

Everyone liked the idea.

Then Matt spoke up. "Guys, if we call everyone in our class to tell them, we'd better remind them *not* to wear a Minnesota Vikings jersey. My sister, Miranda, was in his class and she says he always makes fun of the Vikings."

"Why is that?" Jim wondered.

"It has something to do with the purple jerseys and four lost Super Bowls," Matt replied.

"Tell everyone no Vikings jerseys then," Prez said.

After a few moments, Prez continued, "So, before you guys leave, I'll give you a list of the people I'd like you to call tonight. If any of them don't have a jersey to wear, tell them to wear some type of sports t-shirt or something."

"Sounds good," Charles said.

"Nothing like winning a few brownie points right away," Chad supplied with a big smile.

"One other thing, guys," Prez announced.

"I have a strong feeling that the Governor's announcement tomorrow is going to be a great opportunity for all of us to have a very interesting year. I say we make the best of the opportunity!"

"Now you're sounding a lot like a Presidential candidate," Charles observed.

"Let's just say that I can use all the practice I can get," Prez admitted.

"This is Kerri Andrews, KXMB-TV News. The big mystery tonight is what the Governor of North Dakota will tell the students of our state tomorrow morning at ten o'clock. Right now, I'm standing in front of Maxwell's Books in Kirkwood Plaza with Justin Fischer, who will be a fourth grader at St. Joe's School in Mandan.

"Justin, how do you feel about Governor Ed making a special speech to you kids tomorrow morning?"

"I don't know—I guess it makes me feel kinda special that the Governor wants to talk to just us kids like that."

"Do you have any idea what he might want to talk to you about?"

"My dad and mom think he's going to talk to us about helping him come up with ideas to help keep people from moving out of North Dakota."

"Justin, that sounds like a great idea! Well, whatever the Governor has in mind, he and his staff have kept the content of his message a big secret! It looks like Justin and I and the rest of you will have to wait until tomorrow at ten to find out what he has in mind.

"This is Kerri Andrews, KXMB-TV News, at Kirkwood Mall."

CHAPTER IV

That night I seemed to have weird dreams all night. In one of them, I remember sitting in class, and I knew it was the first day of school. I was sitting somewhere in the middle of the classroom in my desk, and I was very aware that everyone was staring at me. For some reason I didn't recognize anyone in my class, except Troy Aikman, the quarterback of the Dallas Cowboys. I wondered what the heck he was doing in my sixth grade class! When I glanced down at my chest, I was amazed to find I had a Minnesota Vikings jersey on! I couldn't believe it! I knew that I didn't even *own* a Minnesota Vikings jersey, and I was wondering what I was doing wearing one! All of a sudden, everyone started laughing at me! It was humiliating!

In another dream I walked into my classroom on the first day, and I recognized absolutely *no one*! Then everyone started to take out these math assignments, and I was the only one who didn't have mine done! I tried to explain to my teacher, who was some wacky looking guy, that it was the first day of school and we didn't have any homework. Then he started yelling at me, but he was using a language that I couldn't understand. It was a frustrating dream!

When I had homemade cocoa with my parents that morning, I found out that I wasn't the only one who had trouble sleeping that night. My parents said they had some weird dreams, too. It was comforting for me to know that my parents, both of them teachers, got a little nervous about the first day of school. I wondered what kind of dreams Dr. KK might have had last night.

It was a beautiful North Dakota morning that day. The sun was shining brightly with hardly a cloud in the sky. There was no wind whatsoever. Chad came over to my house at fifteen to eight so we could play catch with my football for awhile before we had to go to school. At eight we started walking to Dorothy Moses, only about two blocks from our house.

As we were walking to school, Chad looked at me with a grin on his face and said, "Nice jersey, Kevin." I was wearing my number 15 Nebraska jersey, of course. It was quarterback Tommy Frazier's number.

"Yours is pretty awesome, too, but not quite as great as mine," I said with a big smile. Chad was wearing the identical jersey that I was.

"We've got a new principal this year, don't we?" Chad asked as we crossed Third Street.

"Ya," I answered, "I think my mom said his name is Mr. Messmer. I hope he's half as nice as Mr. Fettig was."

Chad said, "Me, too. Mr. Fettig was the best. I don't think I ever saw him get mad at anyone."

"Me neither," I said, "and it seemed like he knew the names of every single kid at Dorothy Moses."

"Ya, he did," Chad confirmed.

As we approached the fifth and sixth grade entrance to the school, we noticed a man standing by the open doors, shaking the hands of students as they entered the building.

"Speaking of the new principal," I said, "that's got to be him."

I was right. Our new principal, Mr. Messmer, shook our hands, introduced himself, and greeted us with a friendly smile. He said, "Feel free to go to your classrooms and drop off your school supplies and meet your new teachers."

Chad remarked, "I think I'm going to like this guy as a principal."

Dr. KK's room was about halfway down the hall

21

on the right. Before we even entered the classroom, we could see many signs of Dr. KK's love of sports. Almost everything on the walls outside our room had to do with sports. Big letters said, "JOIN A REALLY GREAT TEAM!!" Each of the students in the class had his or her name on a football helmet. Large posters of Larry Bird and The Pittsburgh Steelers hung outside the classroom.

As we walked into the room, the first thing I noticed was that Dr. KK was wearing a number 19 Pittsburgh Steelers football jersey. The next thing I noticed was every kid that was already in the room also had a football jersey on.

Dr. KK saw us enter the room and called from across the room, "Chad and Kevin, come on over here. There's someone I'd like you to meet."

We walked to the other side of the room where Dr. KK was standing with a person who I knew had to be Mike Schaffer, the new student to our school.

Mike had dark hair combed straight back, blue eyes, and a very nice smile. He must have been about two inches taller than me. My first impression was that we were going to get along very well. I also liked the Colorado Buffaloes jersey that Mike was wearing.

After Dr. KK had introduced us to Mike, he said, "Nice jerseys, boys." I had a feeling that our new teacher had caught on to our little plan and loved it!

"Mike," Dr. KK began, "I wonder if you would like to show Chad and Kevin what you showed me when you first came in this morning?"

"Sure," Mike replied. Mike pulled a comb out of his back pocket and began combing his black hair straight back.

All of a sudden, his upper lip started quivering, he swivelled his hips, and said, "Thank you for coming to school this morning. I hope you enjoy the year. Thank you very much." As he spoke, he sounded **JUST LIKE ELVIS PRESLEY**!

"Oh my gosh!" I thought. "This *is* going to be an interesting year!"

CHAPTER V

During the next few minutes, the rest of our sixth grade class wandered in. I've got to admit I felt more than just a little excitement when everyone had arrived. We did have a super-cool class. Something told me that we were in store for an incredible year!

Soon, the last bell rang at 8:30, signalling the official beginning of the first day of school. Dr. KK said, "Welcome to what I hope will be a *great* school year!"

Dr. KK looked around the room at his 23 new sixth graders all wearing football jerseys or sports t-shirts, and a huge smile came to his face. Everyone in the class started looking around the room at everyone else, and smiles were exchanged all over the room. Dr. KK observed, "I sure like the way you people dress!" Everyone laughed, and I knew our little plan was worth the effort.

After that, Dr. KK said, "Before we get started, I need two volunteers to take attendance this week."

Michelle Jaschob and Kris Jaschob, two cute, blonde, identical twins, were chosen to take attendance and record lunch count. Then we said the pledge of allegiance.

Next, Dr. KK said, "I hope you're just as excited as I am about starting another school year! Today should be extra special! As you all know, we're starting this school year with a new principal, Mr. Messmer. How many of you met Mr. Messmer as you were coming into school this morning?"

Almost everyone raised their hand. Then Dr. KK continued talking as he slowly changed his position in the front of the room. "In an hour and a half, we're in for another special event. The Governor of our state is going to speak to all students in North Dakota. I thought we might spend some time talking about what our Governor might have to say that's so important. Let's try to predict what he might be talking about in his message this morning. Any ideas?"

Three people raised their hands right away. Dr. KK called on Krista Nolz. "My sister Kari and I think the Governor wants us to help plan a big party for the year 2000."

"Thanks, Krista," said Dr. KK. "I'm going to write that on the board. It's only a few years until we start the twenty-first century, so maybe the Governor needs our help with ideas to celebrate that event."

"Other ideas?" Dr. KK questioned. He called on Cole Turnbow, who had his hand up.

"My family's talked about this, and we think this has something to do with kids helping to change the lousy way people around the country think about our state."

Dr. KK wondered, "What do you mean by that, Cole?"

"Well," Cole began, "everyone in the United States thinks it's like the North Pole in North Dakota all the time, and many people think we still ride around in covered wagons here and stuff like that."

This comment brought some giggles from the class. Dr. KK asked, "So what could North Dakota kids do to change that image?"

Jenny Kelsch raised her hand and said, "Maybe we could have a poster contest or something showing what the state is really like and show the winning posters to people around the country."

"How could we do that?" Dr. KK inquired.

Prez raised his hand and I got ready for a short speech. Prez stood up and began speaking. "I can think of at least three distinct possibilities," he explained. "First, the winning posters could be placed in newspapers like the *U.S.A. Today*, which are distributed nationwide. Second, the winning posters could be put in other periodicals like magazines. Finally, short TV commercials could be made including these posters."

Mark Hare was called on next. "How about billboards of the winning posters put all over the country?"

Dr. KK smiled and said, "Let me get all these ideas down. Wow, you're all doing a lot of good thinking for the first day of school!"

As Dr. KK was jotting down our ideas, he said, "Any other possibilities?"

Karen Kindem raised her hand. "Yes, Karen," Dr. KK said.

"Dr. KK, I wonder if this message could have anything to do with any of the problems involving kids in Bismarck and in the rest of North Dakota."

"Like what, Karen?"

"Like smoking, for example," replied Karen. "I read in *The Bismarck Tribune* this summer that more young people than ever are smoking in North Dakota."

"Are there any other problems involving kids that the Governor might want to mention?" asked Dr. KK.

Andrea Klein was called on next.

"How about watching too much TV?" she suggested.

"All right," Dr. KK said as he wrote that on the board. "Any more ideas?"

Chad raised his hand and said, "How about not

exercising enough and eating junky stuff?"

"I'll write those down, too," Dr. KK said. "This is great! Do we still have ideas?"

Kari Wise suggested, "This is something like the poster contest, but maybe the Governor is going to let us help design a new license plate for North Dakota."

"All right! We're doing an amazing job!" Next, Dr. KK called on Deirdra Renner.

She said, "How about helping keep young people like my oldest sister in the state after they graduate from college by creating more jobs here in North Dakota?"

"Thanks, Deirdra," Dr. KK said. "I'll get that on the board. Any more ideas?"

At this point, no hands were raised. Dr. KK stated, "You've all done such a good job thinking and participating that I'm going to make a deal with you. If the Governor's message deals with any of the ideas that we've thought of the last few minutes, I'll buy you each an ice cream cone at Hardee's tomorrow. Any objections?"

The rhymer, Blaine Moze, raised his hand, stood up beside his desk, and all of us got ready for his first rhyme of the new school year. He didn't disappoint us as he started talking,

"The Governor will speak,
And my dog likes a bone,
And tomorrow Dr. KK might buy us,
An ice cream cone!"

Everyone laughed!

CHAPTER VI

After a good softball game in my mom's physical education class, we anxiously returned to the classroom to hear Governor Ed speak. Dr. KK already had the television on when we returned from the gym. He had turned off half of the classroom lights so we could all see the TV screen easily.

Soon, Governor Ed appeared on the screen, saying,

"First, I want to thank all North Dakota students and teachers for taking time out on what I'm sure is a very busy first day of school to listen to this message.

"You have so much to be proud of! Your achievement test scores are near the top of all the fifty states. Our high schools can boast of a dropout rate that is among the lowest in our nation. A large percentage of our high school graduates go on to get college degrees. There's no denying that you teachers are doing a great job teaching and you students are doing an extraordinary job learning. For this, we

should be extremely proud!

"At the same time as we can boast of having such an outstanding educational system, there is startling evidence that our state is not doing very well in an area that I believe is just as important as our academic education, and that is our health and fitness!

"Consider these facts. North Dakota is near the top in the country in the percentage of overweight people. Our state leads the nation in diabetes–a disease often resulting from inadequate exercise and poor nutrition. Almost half of you are already developing significant risk factors for heart disease due to lack of adequate exercise and the lack of good nutrition.

"The inadequate fitness in our youth carries through to adulthood. As North Dakotans get older, both their quality and their length of life are affected by their health habits as children. The medical costs because of this are huge!

"I want this to change beginning now. It's time for all North Dakotans to see fitness as a lifetime pursuit, and that's where I need your help. I want the teachers and students of this state, the greatest state in this country, to help me lead a fitness revolution in our state!

"During this school year, I would like you to come up with as many ideas, activities, and programs as possible that help promote and improve the fitness levels of people of all ages in this state! Try them out, and share your best ideas with the rest of us!

"I will be asking the cooperation of all newspapers, television stations, and radio in reporting your progress as the year goes on.

"With your help, North Dakota will become the fitness capital of the country, and all of us will benefit!

"Thank you very much! Have a great day and a super school year!"

Dr. KK turned the television off and Sheree Ternes turned the classroom lights back on.

Blaine raised his hand. Dr. KK called on him, and Blaine stood up and said,

"Tomorrow you will all be,
  At Hardee's with me,
  And Dr. KK will have to buy,
  'Cause he's such a nice guy!"

Everyone applauded, including our teacher.

Dr. KK said, "Congratulations! It looks like I *will* be buying ice cream cones tomorrow. Who was it that guessed what the Governor would talk about, anyway?"

Most of the class looked Chad's way, and chanted,

in unison, "Chad! Chad! Chad! Chad!"

Dr. KK confirmed, "It *was* Chad! And all of you did a *super* job helping predict the content of the Governor's talk! Now, we've got just a few seconds before recess. When we get back in from recess, I think we should talk about what the Governor had to say and what we're going to do about it. Right now, though, let's go out for recess."

As soon as we got in from recess, Dr. KK started leading a discussion about the Governor's speech by saying, "Let's briefly summarize what the Governor had to say in his speech. Who'd like to start?"

Dr. KK called on Jessie Angell. "The Governor said that the people in our state need to get in better shape and he wants us kids and teachers to help."

"That's right, Jessie," Dr. KK said. "Does anyone remember what the Governor would like us to do?"

Nick replied, "Doesn't he want us to come up with ways to get ourselves and others in better shape and then share these ideas with everyone?"

"Uh huh, that's correct, Nick," Dr. KK affirmed. "Does anyone remember some reasons why the Governor said it's so important that we get in better shape?"

Jan raised her hand. "So we can live longer and more healthily."

"All right," Dr. KK began, "does anyone want to add anything else?"

Prez got up from his desk and declared, "Our whole class got together at recess and we'd like to make this a special class project for this year–with your permission, Dr. KK."

"I was hoping you might feel that way," said Dr. KK with a big smile.

"So, how do we get started?" Krista wondered.

Dr. KK responded to Krista's question with a question. "Does anyone have any suggestions?"

Jan suggested, "We might want to do some brainstorming to start out with."

"Ya," Cole agreed, "then when we've got a bunch of ideas, we can develop a real plan of attack."

"Are you students *sure* you're in the sixth grade?" Dr. KK said with admiration.

Then, our teacher thought for a moment and stated, "We'll start brainstorming tomorrow morning. If you have any time tonight, maybe you can start thinking of ideas."

"This is Marci Narum from KFYR-TV News. I'm at Victor Solheim Elementary School in Bismarck today and Governor Ed has just finished making his special announcement to North Dakota students and teachers. I watched the short speech with Darlene Paulson and her second graders. Mrs. Paulson's students, already excited to be back in school, have been even more thrilled by the Governor's special speech and probably the presence of our TV camera.

"A few of Mrs. Paulson's students have volunteered to talk to me about their experience. This is Nick Haugen. Nick, what do you think about Governor Ed's speech?"

"Oh, I thought it was pretty neat."

"Do you think your class is going to help the Governor get North Dakota people in shape?"

"I hope so. I keep in shape by playing football whenever I can."

"That's great, Nick! Who is your favorite football player?"

"I guess it's Barry Sanders from the Detroit Lions."

"He's a great one, Nick!"

"Ya, I even have his rookie football card!"

"That's fabulous, Nick!"

"We've got another second grader to talk to. This is Lindsay Robb. Lindsay, what did you think about Governor Ed's speech?"

"It was fun. Am I going to be on TV tonight?"

"Yes, you are, Lindsay."

"What channel?"

"Uh, Channel 7, Lindsay." (Lindsay seems to be taking over the interview.)

"My dad thinks you're pretty."

"Why, thank-you, Lindsay!" (Marci Narum appears to be blushing.)

"And my mom likes your clothes."

"Well, that's nice of her to say! This is Marci Narum, being interviewed (Marci giggles) by Lindsay Robb, a second grader from Victor Solheim Elementary School in Bismarck!"

CHAPTER VII

Before school was out that first day, a bunch of the boys from our class decided to get together at my house at 7:00 that night to start brainstorming. We found out that several of the girls were meeting at Karen's house at about the same time to do the exact same thing.

When school was out, Chad and Prez and I caught up with Jessie, Karen, Sheree, and Jan in the hall near our classroom. "Hey girls," Prez began, "how late do you plan on staying at Karen's tonight to think about ideas for the Governor's challenge?"

"Until about eight fifteen or so," Karen replied. "Most of us have to be home by eight thirty because it's a school night."

"Would you girls mind if we call you a little before eight so we can share ideas?" Prez asked.

"Good idea," the girls all agreed.

"Kevin, do you have a speakerphone?" Karen wondered.

"Ya, how about you?" I questioned.

"I do, too," Karen replied. "It'll make it easier for everyone to take part in our conversation."

"Great!" Prez exclaimed. "We'll give you girls a call just a little before eight then."

"That gives us only about an hour to brainstorm," Jessie observed.

"That's plenty of time for girls as *brilliant* as we are," Jan said with a grin.

"That just means we won't be able to goof around as much as we usually do," Sheree said with a snicker.

Before anyone arrived at my house that evening, I put the chairs in our family room in a circle. I had some pencils and paper ready if we needed them.

Nine of the eleven boys from our class were able to make it to my house that evening. Nick and Jim weren't able to come because they had some family things to do.

When everyone was comfortable, Prez got things underway. I think he surprised all of us, though, when he looked at Mike and said, "Before we get down to business, would you mind just a little more Elvis Presley for us? I'm a big fan of the King of Rock 'n' Roll."

Mike smiled, and said, "It would be my pleasure." Everyone gave him an enthusiastic round of applause.

Mike stood up, reached into his back pocket, took out his comb, and started combing back his hair. Then his upper lip started quivering and his hips began swivelling just like they had that morning.

All of a sudden, Mike said in his Elvis-like voice, "Thank you. Thank you very much. Now I'd like to sing for you one of my favorite songs called *Hound Dog*."

Mike started singing one of Elvis's greatest hits in a voice that even Elvis would have been proud of, I'm sure!

"You ain't nothin' but a hound dog
    Cryin' all the time..."

His performance was amazing! When he was done, we all clapped with zest, and Mike said, "Thank you very much!"–once again in his Elvis voice, and then he sat down.

"Well, Mike, thank you for your first class entertainment for the evening!" Prez said in a voice that sounded a lot like the President of the United States!

"I guess I'm not the only one who does impressions," Mike noted.

"I'll never reach *your* level of expertise," Prez assured Mike.

Then Prez said, "We've got about forty-five minutes to start coming up with some ideas for our campaign to meet the Governor's challenge." Prez held up a notebook and pen and asked, "Would anyone like to volunteer to be our recorder?"

Mark volunteered. He left his position in the circle and got the notebook and pen from Prez.

"Thanks, Mark," Prez said. "Now, before we start brainstorming, let's try to remember to think *big*. Don't worry how wild or crazy your ideas might be or how much they might cost. Share them anyway. Some of the greatest ideas in history were thought to be completely absurd when they were first suggested. All right, let's begin."

Charles was first to speak, "How about t-shirts?"

Cole added, "Ya, and we'll need a logo and maybe a slogan for our campaign, too."

"Hey!" Matt said excitedly, "We could even have our own fitness song! If we wanted, we could even have Elvis sing it!" This got an enthusiastic response from all of us!

Blaine said, "Ya, I could make sure the song will *rhyme*, at least part of the *time*!"

We all laughed at Blaine's remark!

Mike chuckled and said, "Why not our own blimp! That would get some attention!"

Matt laughed with delight and said, "Somehow the words *fitness* and *blimp* don't go together so well." We all giggled.

I wondered, "How about doing our own fitness show on the Community Access Channel?"

"Ya," Mark agreed, "my dad said anyone can do a program on that channel."

Chad offered, "I wonder if we should educate ourselves more about this whole area of fitness before we do anything like that, though."

"I would agree," Prez said. "But how?"

"My mom says, when you need the best information, consult the experts," Charles observed.

"Great idea," Cole nodded in agreement. "There have got to be many fitness experts in the Bismarck-Mandan area."

"Like your parents, Kevin," Mark said. "They know a lot about fitness and I'll bet they could tell us about a bunch of other people who could help us."

"No doubt," I replied.

"We're doing great, guys," Prez said with a satisfied grin on his face. "I would like to make a suggestion. I think one of the most important things we've got to do is find out why most people in North Dakota *don't* exercise. Then we've got to show them that exercise is not only *important* but also *fun!*"

"Right," I nodded. "Otherwise everything we do isn't really going to make any difference. It would be *really* awesome if we could come up with some ideas that would make North Dakota the fittest state in the country for a long time!"

"That would be phenomenal!" Mike exclaimed.

"Prez," Mark inquired, "how do you think we can get all those people who don't exercise now to want to exercise?"

"I'm not sure, Mark," Prez answered. "But I know one thing. We're going to find out!"

At around five to eight we called the girls. Their brainstorming had centered around one idea that they were really excited about! They thought our class should try to get a fitness float ready for the Folkfest Parade in Bismarck in three weeks!

The Folkfest is a big fall celebration that takes place in the Bismarck-Mandan Community during the last two weeks of September. It includes the Street Fair with great food and crafts, huge yard sales, the Folkfest Queen Competition, and a fantastic parade. The parade and the food are my favorite things.

As soon as Chad and I heard the girls' idea, we both looked at each other, and I could tell we got the same idea at the same time! What if The Starship Exercise was in the Folkfest Parade, too?

Before Prez left my house that night, Chad and I had a chance to tell him about our idea in private. *He loved it*! "Let's go for it!" he exclaimed.

CHAPTER VIII

When Chad and I walked onto the Dorothy Moses playground the next morning at a quarter to eight, some members of our class had already gathered near home plate of the north softball field. Before long, almost our whole class was assembled in that area. The topic of conversation was totally about the Governor's challenge and some of the ideas we had discussed the night before at my house.

When we walked into the classroom, you could feel the tremendous excitement in the air. After attendance had been taken and we said the pledge of allegiance, Dr. KK got a huge surprise when he asked if anyone had thought of any ideas for the Governor's challenge. Almost everyone had a hand raised!

For more than forty-five minutes we shared our ideas, and Dr. KK wrote them on the board. Dr. KK put exclamation points after each idea which I think showed the whole class how he felt about them.

Fitness t-shirts!
Folkfest Parade float!
Fitness logo!
Fitness show on Access Channel!
Fitness song!
Fitness slogan!
Visits by fitness experts!
Find out why most people don't exercise!
Show people exercise is important!
Show people exercise is fun!
Get all ages involved!
Web site on North Dakota Online!

After that, Prez raised his hand and got up out of his desk to tell the class about The Starship Exercise. He said, "Last night after the girls shared their awesome idea about the float for the Folkfest Parade with many of the boys from this class, Kevin and Chad got an idea they told me about. We would like to share that idea with you now. You see..."

Prez told the class about The Starship Exercise and our idea about including it with our class's entry in the Folkfest Parade. While he was speaking, I looked around the room. My classmates' eyes were getting bigger and bigger as Prez went on! Dr. KK looked utterly *amazed*! Soon, he sat down on his stool he called Charlie, and he, too, became wide-eyed, with a huge smile on his face!

When Prez was done, it was completely quiet for several seconds. Finally, Dr. KK said one word, **"AMAZING!"**

Blaine said, "What a *surprise*! The *Exercise*!" Blaine's little rhyme got a pretty good laugh from everyone.

The rest of the morning was devoted mostly to starting to put some of our ideas into action. Jenny said she had talked to her parents about the float idea last night, and they would be happy to give up their garage for the next three weeks so we could build our float there. Jim thought that his grandpa from Mott, North Dakota, would lend us his flatbed for the float. Mike and Cole were confident their dads would help build anything we needed on top of the float. Krista and Karen thought their moms would help organize the rest of the class's moms to help us decorate the float.

Dr. KK said he would work with my mom to schedule some fitness experts to visit our classroom during the next few weeks.

Then Dr. KK noted, "We've got less than three weeks until the Folkfest Parade, so we've definitely got a ton of work ahead of us."

Looking at Prez, he continued, "Prez, do you think

three weeks is enough time for you to test The Exercise adequately?"

"It will have to be, Dr. KK," Prez replied. "I've already got several volunteers to help me out, too."

"Prez," Jan wondered, "where are you going to do your test flights so no one sees what you're doing?"

"My dad says there's a place near Temvik, North Dakota, on one of his friend's land that's virtually isolated. It should be the perfect place for our test flights," Prez answered.

Dr. KK said, "Let me know if I can help in any way."

"I sure will," Prez replied.

Then Dr. KK said, "I think this will be a good time to walk to Hardee's and have those ice cream cones that I owe you. While we're walking, we might want to be thinking about the theme for our fitness float."

Karen observed, "I wonder if we have enough time to get t-shirts made before the parade?"

"If we come up with an idea in the next few days, it should be no problem," Dr. KK assured her.

Cole responded confidently, "We'll have some fantastic ideas before we even get back from Hardee's."

We walked to Hardee's in a line, in pairs, on the sidewalk along Third Street. Chad and I walked next to each other, with Prez and Matt in front of us and Mike and Charles in back of us. After we had crossed the busy Expressway Avenue intersection, Mike suggested, "Guys, we've got to think of a slogan for our float and t-shirts that's catchy and somehow involves The Starship Exercise, too."

After we had walked awhile, Charles suggested, "How about *When you're fit, the sky's the limit!*?"

"Good one," Chad said.

I offered, "How about, *When you're fit, you feel out of this world!*?"

"That'd be cool," Mike said.

Matt said, "We could work the Star Track theme into our slogan like *When you're fit, you can go where you've never gone before!*"

"I like it!" Prez reacted with delight.

In a matter of a few seconds Matt's slogan had been shared with everyone up and down our entire line of walkers, including Dr. KK who was walking with Nick at the front of the line. The response was super-positive."

"As soon as we get to Hardee's," Prez suggested, "we should grab some extra napkins and we'll start designing the t-shirts."

For the rest of the walk to Hardee's, the class started singing songs. First, there was a little of *The Song That Never Ends* and then some *Barney's Theme Song*, and finally some *Silent Night*. Yes, *Silent Night*! (A little weird, I admit!)

When we got to Hardee's, we gathered in a large group in the entry way. Tammy Schmidt, the manager, asked Dr. KK, "What's the special occasion?"

Dr. KK told Tammy about our class having correctly predicted what the Governor's speech would be about.

"I'll tell you what," Tammy said. "I'll buy you each a hamburger and fries to go along with your ice cream cones since you're such a smart class!"

"**Tammy! Tammy! Tammy! Tammy!**" the whole class chanted in unison.

CHAPTER IX

Since the smoking section of Hardee's was totally vacant, our whole class decided to sit there. All the boys were able to fit into two large booths near the back. The girls sat in two other booths close by. Dr. KK was helping pass out the food and was talking to some of his friends who worked at Hardee's.

Later, while we were eating our ice cream cones, Cole already had a pen in one hand and an unfolded napkin on the table. He was drawing the outline of a t-shirt on the napkin, ready to start getting some ideas down on paper.

All of a sudden, out of the nowhere, Mark's big blue eyes lit up and he said, "Hey, wouldn't it be cool if we got Governor Ed to ride on our float during the Folkfest Parade?"

Prez, who was sitting right across from Mark, was so surprised by this great idea that he temporarily lost control of himself and he ended up with the pointed end of his ice cream in his nose!

When the rest of us guys saw Prez with ice cream in his nose, we lost all control, too! As I started laughing, some ice cream came out of my mouth, and a little out of my nose! I wasn't the only one either!

It wasn't long before the girls came over to find out what was going on. Dr. KK wasn't too far behind them, either.

"What's going on?" Dr. KK wondered as he stood next to our booth while several of us were cleaning ice cream from our faces with napkins.

"Sorry, Dr. KK," Prez apologized, "but Mark just came up with what I thought was a great idea that took me completely by surprise. When I stuck my ice cream cone into my nose, the rest of the guys started laughing."

"May I ask what your idea was, Mark?" Dr. KK inquired.

"I just thought it would be neat if we asked Governor Ed to ride on our float with us."

Dr. KK started laughing, and then he said, "That sounds like an idea worthy of ice cream up the nose."

That remark started a major laugh attack by the girls as they continued watching us boys clean up our ice cream mess! Pretty soon, everyone in Hardee's must have wondered what was going on!

When we had settled down, Jim asked our teacher, "Do you think there's a chance the Governor will say yes if we ask him?"

"Who knows?" Dr. KK responded. "And, besides, it never hurts to ask. The worst thing that can happen is he turns us down."

Then Nick spoke up. "Dr. KK, I think I know a way we can increase our chances of getting the Governor to say yes."

"How's that?" Dr. KK wondered.

"If we get the right person to ask Governor Ed, I have a feeling he won't be able to turn us down," Nick replied.

At this point I had no clue what Nick was talking about. Neither did Dr. KK.

Before the day was over, we had called to make an appointment to talk to Governor Ed. We were in luck. The Governor would be able to see us at 3:30 that day!

We found out who Nick thought should ask the Governor to ride on our float. It was Jacy! I had to agree it was a stroke of genius! How could anyone turn down such a *nice* person?

Jacy agreed to ask the Governor, although she was embarrassed that everyone thought she was so *nice*. She wanted Dr. KK and some of the rest of us to go with her, too.

So right after school at 3:00, Dr. KK took Jacy,

Jessie, Chad, and me to the State Capitol where the Governor's office was located. While we were driving north on Ninth Street toward the Capitol in Dr. KK's pickup, we talked about letting Jacy do most of the talking. Jacy even practiced asking Governor Ed to ride on our float.

We arrived at the Governor's office seven minutes before our scheduled appointment, and the Governor's secretary, Naomi, got us each a can of pop to drink while we waited. At almost exactly three thirty, the Governor came out of a door, greeted us, and showed us into his office.

"So, how can I help you?" Governor Ed asked after we had all introduced ourselves and sat down.

Jacy got up from her chair and approached the Governor's desk. "Governor Ed," Jacy began. "Our class is really going to work hard to help make North Dakota the fittest state in the United States."

I looked at the Governor's face and I could tell that Jacy had his full attention.

Jacy continued, "One of our ideas to promote fitness is to build a fantastic float for the Folkfest Parade in a few weeks. What we were wondering was would you consider riding on our float with our class?"

Governor Ed's face suddenly took on a slightly disappointed look, and he said, "Oh, Jacy, I'm so sorry.

I have the Western Governors Conference in Sioux Falls that weekend. I'm afraid I won't be able to do that."

Jacy got an extremely sad look in her eyes, and said, in an almost pitiful voice, "Oh, I'm so sorry, too, Governor Ed, but I guess there's nothing you can do about that. You'll still *always* be my *favorite* governor!"

There was a short pause, and suddenly, the Governor's face changed expression dramatically, as if he had an idea! "One moment, please," he said.

Governor Ed pressed a button on his intercom, and talked to his secretary. "Naomi, check my schedule for Saturday, September 20, and find out what time I'm scheduled to speak at the Governors Conference that day."

In a few seconds, Naomi came on the intercom and said, "Governor Ed, you're scheduled for three."

"Thank you, Naomi," Governor Ed replied.

The Governor looked at Jacy again, this time with a pleasant smile on his face. "Jacy, I think I'm going to be able to ride on your class's float after all. I'll have to fly back from Sioux Falls late on Friday night–so I'll miss the special party that they're having in my honor–but I'll ask the First Lady to take my place–then I'll have to fly right back to Sioux Falls after the Folkfest Parade on Saturday–and the Lieutenant

Governor will have to cover for me during Saturday morning's meetings–but I'm sure she won't mind coming back from her vacation early!"

The Governor seemed almost mesmerized! Then, he asked Jacy, "Is there anything else I can do for you, Jacy?"

"No, Governor Ed! Thanks so much for being such a nice man!"

"Jacy, come back and see me any time!"

CHAPTER X

The next few weeks were super-busy ones! During the school days, we were learning as much as we could about fitness. In the evenings, most of us worked on the float in Jenny Kelsch's garage. On the weekends, we continued working on the float, and some of us helped Prez with his testing of The Exercise.

Several fitness experts visited our class during those three weeks. Before any of these people visited us, we came up with a set of questions to ask them. One of the most important questions that we felt needed to be answered was, *"Why don't most people exercise?"* Another important question was, *"How can we get everyone of all ages involved in an exercise program?"*

We learned so much about so many things from our six visitors. They didn't just talk about *fitness*, they talked about *life*.

Our first visitor was Paul O'Neill, one of the top male gymnasts in the world. Paul is America's best hope for winning a medal in men's gymnastics at the next Olympics. His specialty is the rings, an event that requires a tremendous amount of upper-body strength.

Paul coaches the Dakota Star Gymnastics Club in Mandan. He told us that he thought it was not only important to teach his club members gymnastics, but also to teach them important life skills like the importance of persistence, hard work, and discipline in anything they do in life.

Paul demonstrated his tremendous strength by doing several pushups using just his hands. His feet never came in contact with the floor!

He told us that we can accomplish *anything!* He said, *"You are the only thing that can stop you! GO FOR IT!"*

Melanie Carvell was our second visitor. Melanie is the first and only person from North Dakota to make the Olympic Trials in cycling. She told us that during her race at the Olympic Trials in Colorado Springs, Colorado, she got involved in an awful crash with several other bikes, but she still was able to finish!

Melanie made it clear to us that her husband and three children came first in her life, but fitness was extremely important, too. Besides lots of advice to us about fitness, she had these other four pieces of advice for us:

• We should believe in ourselves!

• When we have a choice, we should take the *hard* way!

• We should tackle the hard stuff first!

• We should set goals and write them down!

Jeff Askew was our next visitor. Before Jeff started answering our questions, he told us about an unbelievable contest he competed in called the Ironman Triathlon. This event, which takes place in Hawaii every year, sounded really tough!

The race starts out with competitors swimming 2.4 miles in the ocean. Once they get done with their swim, the athletes get right out of the water, put on their shoes, and bike 112 miles! Following that, the ones who are still able to go on have to run a marathon, which is 26.2 miles!

Jeff even showed us slides of the Ironman competition that his wife had taken. He told us his wife, Deanna, had also raced in the Ironman Triathlon. Then Jeff passed around the medal he had won for taking part in the race. Jeff also had many things to say about fitness. He gave us these words of advice:

- Chose your friends carefully. Pick friends who will help you be what you want to be!

- Look for the good in everyone!

- Learn not to fear failure. Learn to love trying!

- Whether you think you *can* or think you *can't*, you're probably right!

My mom and her student teacher, Mr. Obenauer, visited us next. Mr. Obenauer is a former pro football player who was doing his student teaching in physical education with my mom. Mr. Obenauer told us about his experience playing pro football over in Sweden for the Stockholm Wildcats.

He said we should study as hard as we can while we're in school, because even if we are able to be a professional athlete some day, that's not a career that lasts very long. Mr. Obenauer thought it was important that everyone get a good education, and he encouraged us to listen to our parents.

Next, my mom explained how she tries to use physical education classes not only to help us learn about the importance of fitness, but also to get a chance to take part in fitness activities that can lead to a healthy lifestyle throughout our lives. She said that just exercising in school is not enough to keep in shape, especially considering the fact that we only have physical education classes three times a week.

Mom told us to "...exercise everyday and appreciate the ability to move. Always say, *I'll try*. Never quit!"

Our last visitor was Myron Cullen, who is an athletic trainer from The Human Performance Center in Bismarck. Myron told us about an exciting training program called the Acceleration Program which has helped many athletes, both amateur and professional, be the best they can be!

He told us about having worked with such great athletes as Phil Hansen of the Buffalo Bills and Chris Carter of the Minnesota Vikings. Myron was a little puzzled when everyone giggled a little and looked back at Dr. KK when the Minnesota Vikings were mentioned.

Myron told us how important it is to keep learning at all stages of life. He told us *to do what we can do to reach our greatest potential!*

After Myron had left, our class decided we would get to work on our own fitness program after the Folkfest Parade, when we had more time to spend working on it.

CHAPTER XI

The Saturday before the Folkfest Parade, Chad and
I wanted to help Prez with his test flight of The
Starship Exercise. When we arrived at Prez's house
before sunrise that morning, Prez and his dad had
already loaded the disassembled Exercise into a large,
double-wide horse trailer. Prez, Chad, and I rode in
the back seat of Prez's dad's blue Blazer for the trip
to the test site near Temvik.

Once we got on the road, Prez wasted no time
getting down to business. "So, guys," he began, "I've
been so busy with The Exercise lately, I haven't had
a lot of time to keep track of all the other projects
we're working on. Catch me up please."

I said, "Well, the float's coming along well, and it
should easily be done by next Saturday."

"Thanks to some really talented parents helping
out," Chad added.

"Ya," I agreed, "there are some fathers who are
expert carpenters, and the mothers know how to

organize the rest of the workers to accomplish tons."

"Like teaching us boys how to make hundreds of tissue flowers to cover parts of the float," Chad said. "By the end of next week, I promise I'll never make a tissue flower again!"

"Never say never," I told Chad with a smile.

Prez asked, "How's *The Fitness Song* coming along?"

"We're letting Blaine and Mike work on that with Deirdra and her mom," I answered. "They say they'll be ready by parade time, too."

"I can just picture it now," Chad said. "Elvis singing our fitness song as our float moves along the parade route."

"With all of us, including the Governor, wearing our beautiful t-shirts," I added. "And with The Exercise flying overhead, too!"

"Speaking of The Exercise," Chad wondered, "are you going to be ready by next Saturday?"

"So far everything's tested out great," Prez said confidently. "If everything goes well today, we're home free!"

I said, "Guys, if everything goes like we plan, the people of Bismarck and Mandan are going to have something to remember for a long time!"

"Maybe some day they'll be talking about this year's Folkfest Parade like my parents talk about the

Blizzard of 1966," Chad observed.

"That would be awesome!" I added with excitement.

When we got to our destination near Temvik, the sun had already risen on what was a perfect, cool, crisp morning. We all pitched together to reassemble The Exercise. Prez grabbed his remote control unit, pushed a few buttons, and soon The Exercise was hovering approximately four feet above the ground.

Prez's dad handed me a yellow object that looked a lot like a calculator the size of a video cassette. A wire was attached to this unit, and at the other end of the wire was a hand-sized disk.

Prez, Chad, and I started walking away from the Blazer along a path of dirt tire tracks through the prairie. Prez's dad stayed with The Exercise.

As we were walking along, I asked Prez, "Are you going to explain what we're doing so I can understand it?"

"I'll try, Kevin," Prez replied.

Prez explained, "Remember those dot-to-dot pages that you used to do where you connected a bunch of dots that were numbered 1, 2, 3, and so forth, and you had to connect the dots in order so they made some sort of picture?"

"I still like to do those, Prez," I said with a smile.

"Well, imagine that every location on earth is one of those dots. What we're trying to do today is create a path of dots for The Exercise to follow. The yellow device that you're carrying, Kevin, gives us some numbers that correspond with each of those dots."

"Where do you get those numbers from?" I wondered.

"They come from a series of satellites out in space called GPS Satellites. That disc attached to the yellow box picks up the number associated with our present location from the satellite closest to us."

"So far I follow," Chad said.

"Anyway, The Exercise is designed to move from one programmed location to the next in the order that I program them into the vehicle's on-board computer."

"So how do you get the data into that computer?" I asked.

"With the remote control unit I'm holding right here," Prez responded. "It serves as a data input device *and* remote control unit."

"So right now we're creating a path of dots for the Exercise to follow?" Chad guessed.

"That's right," Prez answered. "When The Exercise flies away from the position where my dad is right now, we've got to create a path for it to follow. So, how far should we have it fly on its first leg?"

"How about to that tree way over there?" Chad

said, pointing to a large elm tree approximately a half mile straight ahead.

"All right," Prez said, "we'll walk over to the tree and program its position into the Exercise's computer."

I wondered, "How do you make sure The Exercise doesn't fly right into the tree?"

"We have to program a safe altitude for The Exercise to be flying when it gets to that position," Prez answered. "We have to make sure that the altitude is high enough to clear the obstacle."

"I think I get it," Chad said.

"Me too," I said, "except for one thing. Didn't you say before that if you want to, you can fly The Exercise directly using your remote control unit?"

"Yes," Prez answered, "I can maneuver The Exercise very much like people fly remote controlled airplanes you've seen, but the range when I fly that way is only a mile or so. With the *programmed* flight patterns we've been talking about, The Exercise should be able to fly just about anywhere!"

Before we were done walking, we had created a triangular route for The Exercise to follow. It began where the Blazer was parked, proceeded to the large elm tree, continued to an old windmill, and finally returned to the Blazer. We estimated the total distance of our path to be one and a half miles.

When we got back to The Exercise, Prez set the speed for approximately ten miles per hour, and soon The Exercise was off!

CHAPTER XII

"This is Barb Meyer from KFYR-TV News. It's been over two weeks now since Governor Ed challenged the youth of North Dakota to help improve the fitness level of our state. Already, the students of the Bismarck-Mandan area have responded to that challenge.

"Right now, I'm with Ray Heck's sixth grade class from Lewis and Clark Elementary School in Mandan. We've just completed our walk from the school, and we've arrived at The Liberty Heights Senior Citizens Center, approximately six blocks from Lewis and Clark.

"As you'll notice, each of these sixth graders is now meeting up with one or two of the older-than-average residents from here. Then, each of these small groups is going to go for a walk.

"This is Scotty Kiemele, one of the sixth graders. Scotty was the person who came up with the idea of exercising with the residents here. Scotty, just how

68

did you come up with this great idea?"

"Well, we were trying to think of ways to get in better shape that might also help other people, and then I remembered how much I like to walk with my own grandpa, and I guess that helped me come up with this idea."

"How often do you come over here to go for your walks?"

"Well, this is only our second week, but we decided to do this every Tuesday afternoon, at least to start with."

"Thank you very much, Scotty."

"Now, I'd like to talk to Al Kocis. Al is one of Scotty's fitness partners. Al, what do you think of walking with Scotty on Tuesdays?"

"I love it! Scotty's such a fine young man, and we have a good chance to talk about all the fun things going on in his life. It makes me feel younger just being around him."

"Al, do you have any trouble keeping up with Scotty?"

(Scotty approaches the microphone) "Actually, I think Al has to slow down a little from his regular pace so I can keep up with *him*. He's in really good shape for a seventy-nine-year-old guy!"

(Barb Meyer looks astounded but finally speaks) "There's no question about that! I hope I look half as good as you when I'm your age, Al!"

"I'm now talking to Ray Heck, the teacher of this group of sixth graders. Mr. Heck, I wonder what benefits you've already noticed from this activity?"

"One benefit is that the kids are getting some good exercise on a day when they don't have regular physical education classes. The greatest thing I think I've noticed, though, is these sixth graders are making some fantastic friends that they normally never would have had a chance to meet."

"From what I've seen, the residents of Liberty Heights feel the same way about your sixth graders! This is Barb Meyer, about to take a walk with *my* fitness partner from The Liberty Heights Senior Citizens Center in Mandan."

The week before the Folkfest Parade was extremely exciting! I think it reminded me a little of the week before Christmas. On the one hand, I hated to see all the preparation end, because it had been so much fun. On the other hand, I couldn't wait for the day of the Folkfest Parade to finally arrive!

On Tuesday, Deirdra, Blaine, and Mike announced that they were ready to share their fitness song with the class. Deirdra's mom helped make a tape of background music to go along with the song. Deirdra, Blaine, and Mike planned to teach us all *The Fitness*

Song so we could sing it while we traveled the parade route on our float.

Mike left the room for a few minutes to get dressed. When he was ready, Deirdra and Blaine came to the front of the class and said, in unison, *"Ladies and gentlemen! I now give you the King of Rock 'n' Roll, singing a unique fitness song that's been written especially for YOU!"*

When Deirdra and Blaine said *YOU*, Deirdra pressed the *play* button on the tape recorder. Soon, Mike entered the room in a beautiful, all-white, sequined outfit, complete with white shoes! Mike put the lapel of his white sport jacket up, then his lips started quivering and his hips began swivelling just like before. When the music started, *Elvis* began singing the following *Fitness Song* to the tune of *Hound Dog!*

"Well, we're tryin' to get in shape,
  Exercisin' and eatin' right,
Yes, we're tryin' to get in shape,
  Exercisin' and eatin' right,
You can exercise at any age,
  And then you'll all be feelin' right!

When we said we didn't have time,
   Well, that was just a lie,
When we said we were too young or old,
   Ya, that was just a lie,
You can exercise at any age,
   And then you'll all be feelin' right!

Let's get in shape North Dakota,
   Let's exercise and eat right,
Let's stay in shape North Dakota,
   We'll exercise and eat right,
You can exercise at any age,
   And then you'll all be feelin' right!"

Chapter XIII

My mom has told me that the weather for the Folkfest Parade is usually great. That particular Saturday was no exception. With just a few puffy clouds in the sky, a light breeze, and a temperature of approximately 55 degrees, the weather was perfect for a late September morning.

An hour and a half before parade time, Chad, my parents, and I rode over to Prez's house. We wanted to be there when The Starship Exercise started its first public flight.

When we got to Prez's, much of our sixth grade class along with many of our parents had already arrived to witness what we all hoped would be a spectacular event. We weren't disappointed!

Using his remote control, Prez guided The Exercise out of his garage, and soon it was hovering approximately forty feet directly overhead! Many expressions of wonder could be heard from our small crowd as we gazed upward, witnessing the awesome sight!

Then, Prez set the controls so The Exercise would fly at a slow speed straight for the Capitol, where the Folkfest Parade would begin. For a few breathtaking minutes, we watched as The Exercise flew northeast! When it was out of sight, everyone got in their vehicles to head for the Capitol Grounds!

We caught up with The Exercise when we got near The Ground Round, a restaurant on Third Street. As my dad drove slowly, my mom and Chad and I opened the car windows and strained to get the best view of what was an amazing sight!

We noticed that just about everyone else was either looking up or pointing up at The Exercise, too. The bright autumn sun reflecting off the beautiful starship was something to behold!

"Beam me up, Scotty!" I heard someone yell.

My dad increased his speed a little so we'd beat The Exercise up to the Capitol.

We did beat The Exercise by less than five minutes! My dad and most of the other parents from our class parked their cars on the east side of the Capitol Building. Then, my classmates and I ran ahead of our parents to where we knew our float was already parked and waiting.

South of the State Capitol Building is a large rectangular-shaped lawn, wider than a football field and about twice as long. They call this the Mall. An oval-shaped road completely encompasses the Mall. Our float was parked in a huge line of floats on the east side of the oval, near what used to be our State Museum. Many bands were already assembled out on the Capitol Mall, getting ready for the start of the parade.

By the time we got to our float, we could already see The Exercise approaching from the South! Soon, every one of the hundreds of people already gathered at the Capitol Grounds was pointing, yelling, screaming, or just staring at something they'd never seen before! I got a big lump in my throat, knowing that my class and I were part of this!

Prez, now standing next to the float, used his remote control unit to guide The Exercise to a position directly above our float, at an altitude of thirty feet. As people realized where The Exercise was headed, a large crowd soon gathered near our float to watch the approach.

Soon, the Governor of North Dakota made his way to where Prez was standing with most of the class, by the west side of the float. Governor Ed was wearing one of our new fitness t-shirts, and he had a look of exhilaration and surprise on his face!

"I'm sure glad I didn't miss *this*!" Governor Ed exclaimed. "Who's responsible for this anyway?!"

"**PREZ**!" everyone from our class yelled and pointed.

Prez handed the remote control to me, and shook Governor Ed's hand, saying, "Governor Ed, it's *really* a pleasure to meet you! I'm Prez!"

"Are you responsible for that magnificent craft, Prez?" the Governor asked, pointing up at The Exercise.

"I had a lot of help from my friends," Prez replied. "Our whole class and our parents put in a lot of hours working on the float, the t-shirts, and everything else!"

"Well, it's going to be a *real* honor riding in the parade with all of you!" Governor Ed said with an enthusiastic smile.

Suddenly, a bugle sounded a cavalry charge, signalling the start of the parade, and hundreds of people scrambled to get to their starting positions! All of us got into our designated places on the float, and Jenny's dad started his Suburban, ready to pull our float in the parade!

As we drove slowly around the oval toward the exit to Sixth Street, I looked all around me, and then above me to take in all the atmosphere.

Our float and everyone on it looked terrific! We had created a float that was supposed to represent a beautiful planet, called *Planet Fitness!* The float was multi-colored and multi-leveled!

Everyone but Mike had a beautiful new t-shirt on, and many of us were wearing something to represent a particular fitness activity. For example, Governor Ed was wearing his running shorts and shoes, Chad and I had Bismarck Demon football helmets on, and Michelle was doing the splits on what resembled a balance beam. Dr. KK was holding a tennis racket in his hands.

A fluorescent pink sign with black letters clearly identified our float as *Planet Fitness!* Our multi-colored t-shirts said, *Get Fit!* on them. Down near the ground on both sides of the float were letters stating, *"When you're fit, you can go where you've never gone before!"*

At the highest level of the float, Mike was standing in his white sequined Elvis outfit, holding a microphone, ready to lead us in our fitness song. At a level just below the Governor, Prez stood, holding his remote control. I glanced up again and could see The Exercise following us directly overhead, keeping an altitude of thirty feet or so.

CHAPTER XIV

Once we left the oval-shaped road south of the Capitol and began marching down Sixth Street, *Elvis* started singing our fitness song, and the rest of us soon joined him. Prez sang along, but he concentrated most of his attention on maneuvering The Exercise, which was flying less than thirty feet above the top of our float!

Huge crowds lined both sides of the street! When the people heard our fitness song and then sighted The Exercise coming, many of them reacted with excitement, some with surprise, and others seemed almost hypnotized by it all! I'll bet many people were so busy looking at The Exercise, that they hardly even noticed our fantastic float with the Governor of North Dakota and *Elvis* on it!

Our school was not the only one that had entered a fitness float in the parade either. In fact, right in front of us was a colorful float encouraging everyone to eat at least five fruits and vegetables every day. Built

by some students and parents from Pioneer Elementary School in Bismarck, it included huge papier-mache fruits and vegetables, piled high in a large bowl. Many kids and some teachers were riding on the float, too.

As we continued down Sixth Street and then turned right onto Avenue C, the almost deafening cheers continued from the throng gathered to watch the Folkfest Parade. The whole experience was even more exciting than I had imagined! As I looked over at the Governor, I could tell he was enjoying the whole thing as much as the rest of us.

Just when we were about ready to turn south onto Fifth Street, something totally unexpected happened! A huge papier-mache orange, at least six feet high, came rolling off the back of the float in front of us, and rolled straight toward the Suburban that was pulling our float!

Jenny's dad, who was driving the Suburban, was so busy waving to the crowd along the street that he was caught totally by surprise by the huge piece of fruit heading toward him!

When Mr. Kelsch finally spotted the orange approaching him, he hit his brake about the same time as the orange hit his vehicle! The orange harmlessly hit the front of the Suburban and bounced backward. The sudden stop, though, caused a chain reaction!

Michelle fell off the balance beam, onto the back of the Governor, who fell forward, bumping Prez!

Prez stumbled, tried to regain his balance, and dropped the remote control unit onto the street. It shattered into several pieces!

For a few seconds, the whole crowd was quiet, and the parade came to an abrupt halt! The Governor quickly checked to make sure Michelle and Prez were all right. Then Prez jumped down from the float to pick up the pieces of his remote control unit.

A little girl broke the silence as she pointed up into the sky and yelled, "Daddy! The spaceship is flying away!"

That's exactly what was happening! The Exercise seemed to be gaining altitude, and it was flying away from us at a slow speed!

As Governor Ed helped Prez back onto the float, Prez said, "We've got to follow The Exercise!"

Dr. KK asked, "Where do you think it'll go, Prez?"

Prez answered anxiously, "I'm not sure! But would you mind following The Exercise until I can figure something out?"

Governor Ed called out to all of us, "Does everyone want to follow The Exercise?"

"**YES!**" we all answered.

"Let's follow that spaceship!" Dr. KK yelled as we all got back on the float again.

Soon we were riding east along Avenue C, looking

up in the air, trying to follow The Exercise which was traveling who knows where?! When we got to Ninth Street, we noticed that The Exercise seemed to be changing direction! It was now flying northwest, apparently headed back to the Capitol Grounds!

Mr. Kelsch turned north on Ninth Street and we soon caught up with The Exercise. It was now about sixty or seventy feet above us, and it still seemed to be headed for the Capitol Grounds.

"Hey!" Charles yelled as he looked behind us. "Look at the cars following us!"

Most of us had been so busy looking up at The Exercise that we hadn't noticed the long line of cars that had formed behind us, also following The Exercise! It was an unbelievable sight!

Suddenly Prez yelled, "I know where it's going! The on-board computer has switched into one of the pre-programmed flight patterns! It's headed straight for the Capitol!"

Governor Ed yelled back, "Do you mean The Exercise is going to *hit* the Capitol?!!"

"I've programmed it to clear the top of the Capitol by more than thirty feet!" Prez hollered.

We led a line of more than a hundred cars back to the oval-shaped road south of the Capitol. Mr. Kelsch stopped when he got as close to the Capitol as possible!

We had beaten The Exercise back to The Capitol by about two minutes! We all got off the float, and stood and watched The Starship Exercise approach from the South! Hundreds of other people who had followed us up to the Capitol watched with us!

As The Exercise flew above the large lawn toward the Capitol, I could tell it wasn't flying high enough to clear our eighteen story Capitol Building! Someone in the crowd even yelled, "It's going to hit the Capitol!"

Most of the crowd, however, was quiet as they watched, photographed, or videotaped the incredible sight of The Exercise slowly approaching the Capitol, seemingly gaining altitude, but still on a collision course to hit the side of the building!

As The Exercise got within a hundred yards of the Capitol Building, everyone seemed to hold their breath as the spaceship slowly approached–slowly gained altitude–and then **CLEARED THE TOP OF THE CAPITOL!**

When The Exercise had successfully cleared the top of the Capitol, the crowd that had gathered let out a huge cheer!

CHAPTER XV

Governor Ed, Dr. KK, Mr. Kelsch, some of the other parents, and all of our sixth grade class were gathered near the float. "Prez!" the Governor called, "Where is The Exercise headed next?"

"If everything works right, it should fly over Northridge Elementary School next, then over Grimsrud School, and then over to Mandan!"

"Then where?" Dr. KK wondered.

"Then it should fly over The Mandan Refinery, and then over Mandan High School. After that, it'll fly along Mandan's Main Street, and down to Ft. Lincoln State Park to the Custer House. Finally, it should fly over the Missouri River back to my house."

"Will it land at your house then?" the Governor inquired.

"It would if my remote control was operating," Prez explained.

"I'm really sorry about that, Prez," Governor

Ed said, feeling a little responsible for breaking the remote control unit.

"It wasn't your fault, Governor Ed," Prez said. "It was just an accident."

The Governor asked Prez, "Speaking of the remote control unit, how long would it take for you to make another one?"

"About a day, if I had all the materials on hand," Prez explained.

"So, what's going to happen when The Exercise gets to your house without your remote control?" Governor Ed wondered.

"The Starship Exercise *should* move into its next pre-programmed flight pattern," Prez replied.

"And what *is* its next pre-programmed flight?" Dr. KK asked.

"It's a tour of North Dakota," Prez announced.

"Do you mean The Exercise is capable of flying around the entire state?" Governor Ed looked amazed.

"Yes, sir," Prez said confidently.

"So what do we do next?" Mr. Kelsch wondered.

"I say we follow that spaceship!" Dr. KK suggested. "As long as it keeps moving at a slow speed, we all should be safe riding on the float!"

"All right!" Matt Bitz yelled with delight. "Let's follow that starship!"

"EXERCISE! EXERCISE! EXERCISE!" all

of us sixth graders hollered with delight.

Mr. Kelsch said, "I've got a cellular phone in my Suburban so we can call the parents that aren't here to let them know what we're doing."

"I've got an idea!" Governor Ed began. "My house is just a half block from here. Prez, why don't you run over to my house with me. We'll get my car and follow behind the float and try to figure out what to do next! I've got a cellular phone and State Radio right in the car if we should need it! I'll have to call the First Lady and let her know I might be late getting back to Sioux Falls, too."

"Governor Ed, could Jacy, Kevin, and Chad come along with us?" Prez asked.

"If it's all right with your teacher and your parents," Governor Ed replied.

"It's OK with me," Dr. KK said.

Chad, Prez, Jacy, and I ran over to the Governor's house while everyone else got back on the float.

When Governor Ed said we were going to get his *car,* I sort of expected that he would have a Cadillac or something. Did we ever get a *huge* surprise when the Governor opened up his garage door! Inside was a pink Model A with the license plate **PINKY 1**!

Chad and I got to ride in the rumble seat in the back, while Jacy and Prez got in the front with Governor Ed.

"This is Phil Parker!"

"And I'm Mark Armstrong from KFYR-Radio in Bismarck. Less than an hour ago Phil and I were riding in the K-Fire Cruiser in the Folkfest Parade. Right now, we're still in the K-Fire Cruiser, but now we're involved in a whole different kind of parade. This parade is following The Starship Exercise as it flies over the Bismarck-Mandan area."

"That's right, folks, Mark and I are *not* kidding! We're near the front of a line of what I would estimate to be at least several hundred cars, floats, fire trucks, and other vehicles traveling at a speed of approximately twenty miles per hour on The Refinery Road near Mandan. The Starship Exercise is traveling at the same speed and is approximately 200 yards to our right at an altitude that I would estimate to be around sixty feet or so. Wouldn't you say that's about right, Mark?"

"I would agree, Phil! I might add that The Exercise is now flying over the huge storage tanks that Bismarck-Mandan residents are so familiar with! It really is an incredible sight!"

Phil said, "I guess we should try to explain the story behind this amazing scene so our listeners won't think we're completely nuts or playing some sort of practical joke!"

Mark continued, "That's right. Here's what we've heard so far. We understand that The Exercise was built by a sixth grader from Bismarck but that hasn't been confirmed. We've also been told that The Starship Exercise was part of an entry in the Folkfest Parade from Dorothy Moses Elementary School."

Phil added, "As I understand it, The Exercise was flying over a float when it somehow got away! We've also been told that the Governor was riding on the float along with an Elvis impersonator!"

Mark said, "We're not making any of this up, either, ladies and gentlemen! The Governor was supposedly riding on the float because the float was somehow promoting fitness in response to the Governor's challenge to the kids of North Dakota that was made at the beginning of the school year!"

Phil observed, "We've even been told by one caller that the Governor is somehow responsible for the Exercise flying on its own!"

"So far, Phil, we've seen The Exercise fly over the Capitol, then over the Northridge Elementary School area, and then right over Grimsrud Elementary School."

" Yes," Phil began, "and after that, it pretty closely followed the Interstate over the Grant Marsh Bridge, then here to the Refinery. It now seems to be headed toward the north part of Mandan!"

Mark pleaded, "Folks, you can help us out here! If you know anything more about this truly incredible story, please give us a call here in the K-Fire Cruiser. We can be reached at 1-888-5555. We intend to follow this story to its conclusion."

"Yes, Mark and I will follow The Exercise wherever it may go—as long as doesn't switch into *stardrive* or something!"

CHAPTER XVI

PINKY followed right behind our fitness float as it moved down Sunset Drive in Mandan, approaching Mandan Senior High School. Off to our right, The Exercise flew at an altitude of less than fifty feet, providing another breathtaking view for all of the observers!

The caravan of vehicles following The Exercise now numbered more than five hundred! It extended several miles behind the leaders. The fitness float and **PINKY** were near the front of the long line. Twenty vehicles behind **PINKY**, Phil and Mark continued to report from the K-Fire Cruiser.

Soon, the driver of the Camaro driving behind **PINKY** started honking!

Chad said, "Governor Ed, two people in the car are waving, trying to get our attention!"

"Maybe they just want to say hi to **PINKY** and us!" the Governor guessed.

"No, I think they're trying to tell us something," I

said as I watched the people in the Camaro open their front windows.

Then, we heard them yell, "Turn your radio on to KFYR!"

"We will!" Chad said as he and I rode comfortably in the rumble seat.

The Governor turned the radio on, found 550 on the AM dial, and we heard:

"Our Starship Exercise Caravan is getting longer and longer. We've had calls from people who claim they are in this line and they're still back in Bismarck near Econo Foods. That's more than six miles from here!"

"Yes, Phil, this story is getting bigger by the moment! We even had a person recently call and claim that the Governor is not too far ahead of us in the caravan and that the fitness float he was riding on in the parade is right in front of his car."

"But, then again," Phil admitted with a giggle, "we've also had a caller who claimed that he saw Santa Claus peeking out of The Exercise!"

"That's true!" Mark agreed, "However, Governor Ed, if you are listening to us now, please give us a call. We would like to talk to you. We also urge anyone else who has any information about The Exercise or this unique caravan to call us at our toll free number 1-888-5555."

"Are we going to give Phil and Mark a call?" Jacy asked Governor Ed.

"Prez, why don't you make the call," the Governor suggested as he handed his cellular phone to Prez, who then dialed the number.

"This is Phil Parker. You're on the air."

"Phil, this is Prez. I'm calling from **PINKY** near the front of the caravan. I'm the sixth grader mostly responsible for The Starship Exercise."

"Hi, caller, this is Mark Armstrong. You say your name is Prez, and you're calling from **PINKY!**" I could tell Mark thought he was getting a prank phone call.

"Mark," Prez said, "**PINKY** is the name of Governor Ed's pink Model A! I'll let you talk to the Governor right now. He's right here next to me."

Prez handed the phone to Governor Ed. "Hi Mark! Hi Phil! This is Governor Ed!"

"Well! Hi Governor!" Mark said with surprise in his voice.

"Hi Governor!" said Phil Parker. "How are you doing?"

"I'm having a great time!" Governor Ed replied.

"Where exactly are you, anyway?" Mark wondered.

"Well, right now we're going past Mandan Senior

High School. The Exercise is presently flying over the high school. It's quite a sight!"

"Governor Ed," Mark began, "we must be about two blocks behind you on Sunset Drive. Our view of The Exercise is not as good as yours, but it's still quite spectacular!"

"Phil and Mark," Governor Ed said, "I'm going to hand the phone back to Prez. I don't like talking on my phone while I'm driving, and Prez knows much more about all this than I do."

The Governor handed the phone back to Prez.

"Prez, this is Mark again. Please forgive me if I seemed skeptical about your call at first."

"That's fine," Prez said. "This whole situation is quite unusual."

"That it is!" Mark agreed. "Prez, would you like to tell our listeners about The Exercise and how you met up with the Governor."

"Well, The Starship Exercise and our fitness float, which is right in front of us at this very moment, were both meant to promote improved fitness for all North Dakotans. Mark Hare, who's in our sixth grade class, thought it would be great if we asked Governor Ed to ride on the float, since it was the Governor's idea to get North Dakotans in better shape."

Phil asked, "So how did The Exercise get away from your float?"

"Actually, we had a little accident while we were on the parade route, and my remote control unit got broken."

Mark inquired, "So are you saying The Starship Exercise is flying out of control?"

"Not exactly. It's now flying a path that I've already programmed into the on-board computer."

"Prez," Phil supplied, "this is fascinating. Could you tell us where The Exercise is headed next?"

"Well," Prez explained, "if everything goes the way I expect..."

CHAPTER XVII

"Folks, this is Phil Parker along with Mark Armstrong reporting from North Dakota's own Starship Exercise Caravan. We're running out of adjectives to describe some of the sights we've seen in the past couple of hours!"

"That's right, Phil! I thought seeing The Exercise fly over the top of the Capitol Building was incredible, but a few moments ago, we watched The Starship Exercise fly at a low altitude right over Cavalry Square here at Fort Abraham Lincoln south of Mandan. Then it flew directly over the house of George Armstrong Custer."

"It was quite a sight, Mark! I wonder what George and Libbie Custer would have said if they were still here?"

Mark said jokingly, "George probably would have thought that it was just Sitting Bull doing reconnaissance on him!"

Phil added, "Ya, maybe George wouldn't have gone

on to the Little Bighorn if he thought Sitting Bull had the technology to build a starship!"

"Right, Phil!" (They both laughed!)

Phil announced, "Now, radio listeners, we have another Kodak moment to tell you about. The Exercise has just changed direction and is about to fly in a northeasterly direction over the beautiful Missouri River, just like Prez told us it would."

"Yes, Phil, those of us who live in North Dakota often joke about the lack of scenery in our flat prairie state, but even without The Exercise being here, this is a breathtaking view! With The Exercise included, it's absolutely spectacular!"

Phil observed, "The Starship Exercise seems to be headed for Prez's house in South Bismarck near Dorothy Moses School, just like Prez said it would. After that, if things keep going the way Prez told us they should, The Starship Exercise is off to Jamestown, then Fargo, Grand Forks, Devils Lake, Rugby, Minot, Williston, Beach, Medora, Dickinson, and then back to Bismarck!"

Mark added, "And, by that time Prez hopes to have another remote control device ready so he can land The Exercise safely at his home."

Phil asked, "How long did Prez say it would take The Exercise to make the big tour of North Dakota?"

Mark replied, "Well, as soon as The Starship

Exercise gets out of Bismarck, he said it increases its speed to about 50 miles per hour, so he estimates 17 hours for the complete tour."

"And ladies and gentlemen, Mark and I plan to stay on the air during that entire flight to keep you informed of what's going on! We'll have open phone lines, too. We hope to be periodically talking to Governor Ed and Prez and anyone else that wants to talk about fitness or this historic Starship Exercise Caravan!"

"Speaking of this caravan, Phil, the people back in the studio are telling me that the national networks are already calling our station to learn more about this whole thing!"

"Fabulous, Mark! I always wanted to meet Connie Chung!"

As Governor Ed, Jacy, Prez, Chad, and I drove in the Governor's car, headed for Prez's house, we were listening to Phil and Mark on the radio and glancing off to our right, watching The Exercise. In front of us, Dr. KK and the rest of our class continued their adventurous ride on our fitness float.

"Governor Ed?" Jacy asked in her sweetest voice. "Do you think there's any way our whole class can tour the state with The Exercise?"

"I don't know," the Governor began. "When The Exercise speeds up to 50 miles an hour, it wouldn't be safe to ride on the float. Also, much of the trip is going to occur in the dark when it gets pretty cold."

"I wish there was some way our whole class could follow The Exercise around the state together," Jacy said. She was melting Governor Ed's heart once again.

"Maybe there is a way!" the Governor exclaimed. "Hand me the phone, will you, Prez?"

CHAPTER XVIII

In an hour, Governor Ed had a charter bus parked in front of Dorothy Moses School. All the students from our class, many of the parents, Dr. KK, and Governor Ed were anxious to join The Starship Exercise Caravan on its North Dakota Tour!

Chad, Nick, Matt, and I helped Prez load five boxes of materials on board so he could work on building another remote control. Prez began setting up shop in the back of the bus.

Many of the parents carried on coolers filled with food and soft drinks. Several radios, cam corders, and even a few TVs were carried on board.

The only problem we had once we got under way was catching up with The Exercise! It was already more than twenty miles ahead of us on its way to Jamestown!

Governor Ed came through for us again, though. Thanks to an escort by six North Dakota Highway Patrol cars that led us down the passing lane of

Interstate 94, we were able to catch up with the last car in the caravan fifty miles west of Jamestown. We had to pass hundreds of cars, however, before we got to the *front* of the caravan.

Once we got there, the Highway Patrol cars guided us into the right lane of the Interstate. After that, the six patrol cars remained in a line right in front of us, lights flashing! It looked like we were getting an official escort!

As we looked out the windows in front of the bus, we could see The Starship Exercise flying above us at an altitude of approximately 50 feet! What a sight it was! Everyone in the bus applauded!

"This is Phil Parker!"

"And I'm Mark Armstrong reporting LIVE from near the front of The Starship Exercise Caravan! Just a few minutes ago, the Governor created a huge amount of excitement when six North Dakota State Highway Patrol cars led a bus in which he was traveling to the front of our caravan! We understand that several other Highway Patrol cars are in the passing lane all the way along the length of this caravan to help ensure its safe movement through the state!"

Phil asked playfully, "Doesn't this kind of make you feel important and special, Mark?"

Mark said, "Yes, it gives me tons of warm fuzzies, too."

Phil continued, "Right now, we're trying to reach the Governor on his cellular phone–I think we now have him on the line–Governor Ed, are you there?"

"Yes, I am! We're happy to finally have caught up with you and The Starship Exercise!"

"Governor, this is Phil Parker, you sure know how to make a dramatic entrance!"

"Well, thanks! I'm happy to have all the sixth graders from Dr. KK's class and many of their parents with me, too!"

Mark said, "Governor, I think we're just about to have another Kodak moment! It looks like two National Guard helicopters are heading toward The Exercise! You don't have anything to do with them being here, do you, Governor?"

"I may be guilty! I thought both a land *and* an air escort was a good idea! I'm glad the National Guard agreed with me!"

Phil observed, "It looks like the helicopters are moving a mile or so ahead of The Exercise and are maintaining approximately the same altitude as the Starship! This is truly a spectacular sight!"

Governor Ed exclaimed, "It really is!"

Mark said, "Governor, for the next sixteen or so hours we hope to try to report on the movement of this caravan–the people riding with us around the state and the places we go. I know that many of our callers will have questions for you, Prez, and some of the other people on your bus. But we want to do one more thing that I think is probably just as important. We'd like to have our listeners call in and comment, ask questions, and help us discuss the real purpose of The Starship Exercise–to promote the improved fitness of the people of North Dakota."

Governor Ed replied, "That would be great! I've got three extra batteries for my phone so we can stay on the line with you nonstop! All of us riding here in the bus will stay tuned to KFYR during the entire trip, and we'll be happy to contribute in any way we can to your discussion of fitness!"

Mark requested, "Governor Ed, I wonder if you could hand the phone to Prez for just a minute."

"OK, Prez is pretty busy at the back of the bus right now, but I'll see if he'll talk to you briefly..."

"Hi, this is Prez."

"Prez, this is Mark Armstrong. Thanks for taking the time to talk to us. We won't keep you long. I'm sure our audience is all wondering how it feels to have your creation, the beautiful Starship Exercise, getting the attention of the whole state!"

"I guess I'm so busy thinking about getting another remote control unit built before we get back to

Bismarck that I haven't had any time to think about that."

Phil asked, "Prez, what will happen if you don't accomplish that?"

"I prefer to think positively. I *will* have another remote control unit built before we get back to Bismarck."

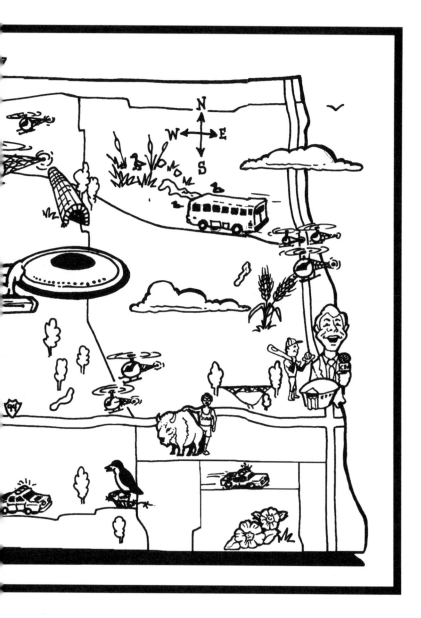

CHAPTER XIX

What excitement we experienced as our caravan continued to move east along Interstate 94, following The Exercise with its helicopter escort! Several radios on board the bus were tuned to KFYR radio, as Phil and Mark reported the latest news regarding this amazing event!

There was almost a party atmosphere on board the bus. Prez, however, was working on building his remote control unit in the back of the bus. Occasionally, he'd take a break to watch The Exercise, and talk with some of us. Then, he'd go right back to work. The noise on the bus didn't seem to bother him a bit.

Several big highlights occurred the next hour. When we got to Jamestown, we got to watch the helicopters, and then The Starship Exercise, fly low over the world's largest buffalo in Jamestown! Hundreds of people were standing near the base of the buffalo, including Rollie Greeno, a great coach from Jamestown College. Coach Greeno called Phil and Mark and we listened to the conversation in the bus.

"Coach Greeno, it's great to have you on the line!" Phil exclaimed.

"It's all my pleasure! It's not every day we see something like this in Jamestown!"

Mark said, "Coach Greeno, I know as coach at Jamestown College in track, football, cross country, and wrestling, your athletes have always been some of the best conditioned athletes anywhere. But I've heard that your own personal fitness is also extremely important to you."

"Actually, Mark, there was a point in my life where I was getting heavy and out of shape when I decided it was time to either make some changes or my health would be at risk. That's when I decided to start jogging."

Phil asked, "Is there anything you would like to tell all of our listeners out there, Coach?"

"I guess I would like to tell all of those who are going to be starting an exercise program to persevere! You're going to have some times when you're probably going to want to quit, but just keep going! It's worth the effort! Also, try to find a fitness activity that you enjoy! Getting in shape and staying there can really be fun if you find activities that you look forward to doing!"

Mark said, "Coach, thanks so much for calling us!"

"Thank-you! And special thanks to the Governor and Prez and everyone else on the bus for promoting fitness in this state! I'll be listening to you guys on the rest of your trip! Good luck!"

Phil replied, "I know everyone in the bus is listening and we all appreciate those remarks, Coach Greeno!"

After driving thirty-two miles more to the east, we approached the town of Valley City.

"This is Phil Parker! We're coming up on another unbelievable sight! We're about to drive down into the large valley that is the site of the town appropriately named Valley City! The two helicopters are about to fly over the long railroad bridge that most North Dakota residents know as the Hi-Line Bridge. The Hi-Line Bridge spans much of this beautiful valley."

Mark Armstrong observed, "It looks like there are several people standing up on the bridge waving as the helicopters and The Exercise go by! They'd better hope a train doesn't come by soon!"

Phil noted, "Either way, this is going to be a moment they'll *never* forget!"

On the sixty mile stretch from Valley City to Fargo, Phil and Mark took calls from all over the state.

Phil said, "Well, let's take some calls now as we continue this fitness caravan on its way to North Dakota's largest city, Fargo."

"Hi, this is Erica Nathan from Valley City!"

Phil said, "Erica, we just passed you in Valley City! Did you get in on all the excitement?"

"I sure did! It was awesome!"

"What would you like to say, Erica?" Phil asked her.

"I'd like to ask Governor Ed a question about fitness."

"Go ahead," Phil said. "He's listening and he can talk on the radio from the bus using his cellular phone."

"Well, Governor Ed, my English class at Valley City High School has interviewed a lot of people the past few weeks about why they don't exercise, and most of them say they just don't have enough time. What would you say to them?"

Governor Ed responded, "Erica, that's a great question. Many people are very busy, some have two jobs and a family to take care of, and I know how difficult it is to find time to exercise. I guess I would tell those people this. I believe that no matter how busy we are, we should be able to find at least twenty to thirty minutes three to five times a week to exercise. Our bodies need that much exercise to work well! I think if everyone takes a close look at their schedules during the week, they can find that much time for something that is so important."

Mark wondered, "Governor Ed, how often do you find time to exercise on your busy schedule?"

"I love to run, Mark, and I find the time to run about 35 miles a week. I'd like to mention one more thing, too! I think that those of us who do exercise find out that we are able to find more energy for the things we need to do during the day, because we're helping our body stay in good condition."

Phil added, "I think studies now show that exercise increases *length* of life, too, not just *quality* of life!"

Governor Ed agreed, "That's right, Phil. It really doesn't take much of a time commitment to keep your body working well. Twenty or thirty minutes three to five times a week is a good investment in your life."

Erica said, "Thanks, Governor Ed!"

"Thank you, Erica!" Governor Ed replied.

Phil continued, "Let's take another call."

"Hi, this is Joey Eberle from Williston."

"Where do you go to school, Joey?" Phil wondered.

"I'm a junior at Williston High School," Joey replied.

Mark asked, "What's your question, Joey?"

"I just wanted to share an idea that my phy. ed. class came up with to help promote fitness."

"Go ahead, Joey," Mark said.

"Well, we interviewed people, too, and we found out that a lot of people start exercise programs, but then they quit, usually after a few months, sometimes even after just a few weeks. Our class thought that having a fitness expert to keep in touch with when you're starting an exercise program could make a big difference to help keep people motivated and everything."

Governor Ed said, "Joey, that's a super idea! Did your class come up with a way to help people get in contact with the fitness experts?"

"Ya, we thought someone should put a list of the experts in each type of fitness activity on North Dakota Online with their E-mail addresses and regular addresses and phone numbers and stuff so they could be contacted easily. We also thought that the list could maybe be put in the paper and maybe even in a special place in the phone book."

"Great idea, Joey!" Governor Ed said. "I myself find it really helpful talking to other runners, so I can see how helpful that would be for people just starting an exercise program."

Phil said, "Joey, we'll be coming through Williston at around one o'clock tomorrow morning! Are you going to be awake to see us?"

Joey answered, "I wouldn't miss it!"

"Then we'll see you later," said Phil.

Mark observed, "We've already had some terrific ideas! Let's take another caller. Hello!"

"Hi, I'm Erica Kubik and I'm a fifth grader at McKenzie School. I just wondered if you could have Elvis and everyone else on the bus sing *The Fitness Song!*"

Mark asked, "Governor, did you people on the bus hear that request?"

"Yes, we did!" the Governor replied. "I'm getting Elvis over here closer to my phone so he can lead us—here we go..."

CHAPTER XX

Just five miles outside of Fargo, we heard on the radio that Tom Broklow from NBC News had heard about our caravan while he was vacationing in South Dakota's Black Hills and had flown to Fargo to join us! He planned on meeting up with us at the Fargodome, a huge indoor sports arena on the campus of North Dakota State University in Fargo.

When the people of Fargo found out that The Starship Exercise Caravan was coming, they lined the streets in huge numbers. There was a definite parade atmosphere as our caravan moved through the streets, and the helicopters and The Exercise flew overhead! Luckily, Prez had programmed The Exercise to fly at a speed of 20 miles an hour over the city of Fargo so we could keep up!

Before we got to the Fargodome, Chad asked me, "Kevin, do you think we'll ever get a chance to play football in the Fargodome?"

"Yup," I replied, "when we play for the State High

School Football Championship with the Bismarck Demons!"

"Would you ever want to play college football at North Dakota State?" Chad wondered.

"Never, Chad! We're both going to Nebraska!"

"Never say never, Kevin!" Chad said.

Chad changed the subject and asked, "Didn't Roger Maris, the famous New York Yankee baseball player, grow up here in Fargo?"

Governor Ed overheard our conversation, and answered, "That's right! Roger went to Fargo Shanley High School!"

I wondered, "How many home runs did he have in one year again?"

Governor Ed replied, "In 1961 he had 61 home runs! 61 in '61! That's an easy way to remember it!"

"Maris broke Babe Ruth's record, didn't he?" Chad asked.

"That's right," Governor Ed said. "It was a record many thought never would be broken, but a great North Dakota athlete proved them wrong."

When we got near the Fargodome, we noticed Tom Broklow and a film crew. Tom was talking as the crew was filming the two helicopters and The Starship Exercise as they flew over the huge domed stadium! What an unbelievable sight!

Soon, the caravan stopped briefly as we picked up Tom Broklow and the two people on the film crew. As the Governor and everyone else greeted Tom when he stepped on our bus, Mr. Broklow said, "When I heard about this on the radio, I just knew I had to see it myself! Now, I'm glad I came!"

Before long, Tom was interviewing Prez in the back of the bus. Meanwhile, our caravan was heading north on Interstate 29 toward Grand Forks, North Dakota. Phil and Mark continued to talk on the radio.

Phil reported, "Hey, we now have another famous person riding on the Governor's bus! A few minutes ago, we saw Tom Broklow of NBC News getting on board! We understand he's quite busy right now, but we'll try to interview him later. Right now, let's take another call. Hello!"

"Hi, I'm Alexis Guzman from Grand Forks."

Mark asked, "Where do you go to school, Alexis?"

"I'm in Mrs. Bethke and Miss Crawford's fifth grade class at Carl Ben Eielson School at the Air Force Base here."

"What would you like to say, Alexis?" Mark inquired.

"I have two questions. First, is The Starship Exercise going to fly over the Air Base, and second, I'd like Governor Ed to tell me why all schools in

North Dakota don't have phy. ed. classes everyday to help the kids get in better shape?"

Mark said, "Alexis, I can answer that first question because Prez has told us that The Exercise will be flying over you in less than half an hour. As far as the second question goes, we'll let the Governor answer that. Governor Ed, are you there?"

"Yes, I am, Mark. I'm not sure why all students don't have physical education classes each day in our state, but I certainly think that's something to take a close look at. I'll find out about that as soon as I get back to Bismarck."

Phil noted, "We have another caller on the line. Hello!"

"Hi, my name is Mike Kern and I'm a third grader from Sweetwater Elementary School in Devils Lake. I was wondering if we're going to be able to see The Starship at all when it goes over Devils Lake?"

Mark said, "Hey, Mike! I think I can answer that question. It's going to be between eight and nine o'clock at night before we get to Devils Lake and it will be completely dark. However, Prez has told me that the red, white, and blue lights that will illuminate The Exercise will make an incredible sight! Along with the helicopters flying low overhead, the hundreds of cars with their headlights on, and the flashing lights from all the Highway Patrol cars, you should see an amazing show, Mike!"

"Oh, great!"

"We have another caller on the air. Hello!" Phil said.

"Hi, I'm Darrin Johnson from Pioneer Elementary School in Bismarck. Our float was the one that the big orange fell off and caused Prez to break his remote control!"

"Darrin, you don't feel responsible for the accident, do you?" Mark asked.

"Well, sorta. You see, I was the one who taped and stapled the orange down to our float!"

Prez heard this conversation and ran to where the Governor was holding his cellular phone near the front of the bus! "This is Prez, Darrin!"

"Hi, Prez, I'm sorry about breaking your remote control!"

"Darrin, the whole thing was just a weird accident. Don't worry about it! Actually, I'm glad the accident *did* happen! This caravan is a real blast! I was just interviewed by Tom Broklow! I've gotten to be good friends with Governor Ed! It really doesn't get much more exciting than this!"

"Thanks for being so understanding, Prez!"

"Thank-you for being so honest, Darrin!"

Mark said, "It sure is great to meet so many outstanding young people! Prez, before you go back to your work, we have another caller on the line that's a special friend of yours!"

"Hello, Prez, this is Betty Haaland from the Espresso counter at your favorite Dan's Supermarket Store. Are you going to be in tomorrow for your usual decaf mocha?"

"Yes, Betty, if you promise to put a little extra whipped cream on it for me. The Exercise should land at my house at around 7 a.m. tomorrow morning, and I'll be over there for my mocha by eight."

"I'll see you then, Prez!" Betty said. "Good luck the rest of the way!"

"Thanks, Betty!"

CHAPTER XXI

By the time we approached Grand Forks, it was beginning to get dark outside. The Starship Exercise Caravan with its land and air support began to put on a light display that was out of this world! Then, we got another surprise!

Suddenly, three big United States Air Force helicopters from the Grand Forks Air Force Base joined the other two helicopters in formation ahead of The Exercise! It looked like the Air Force wasn't going to let the National Guard have all the fun!

The darker it got, the more spectacular the sight became! In the air there were five well-lit helicopters leading the beautifully illuminated Exercise with its red, white, and blue lights. On the ground, there were hundreds and hundreds of vehicles in a line, headlights beaming, led by six North Dakota Highway Patrol cars with lights flashing. Up until that time I had thought the Fantasy of Lights Parade at Disneyworld was the most beautiful display of lights I had ever seen. Our caravan, though, was much more spectacular than that!

To add to this light show, something else began to happen! Along Highway 2, people stood on the side of the road holding flashlights or lanterns. When we drove through Devils Lake and Rugby, there were so many people doing this that it almost seemed like we were driving through a tunnel of lights!

Meanwhile, Phil and Mark helped Tom Broklow and his crew make a video satellite link to the K-Fire Cruiser. Every half hour after that, Mr. Broklow made live television reports about our caravan to the whole country!

As we neared the city of Minot, Tom Broklow filed this live report.

"This is Tom Broklow with this special report for NBC News. A few weeks ago, the Governor of North Dakota challenged the young people of his state to help get the residents of the state in better physical shape. I'll bet he never thought that his challenge would lead to this!

"The picture you're now viewing should give you a sample of the overwhelming sight that those of us who are traveling in this caravan are enjoying! I've covered big news stories all over the world, and I've never seen anything like this!

"Right now, I'd like to talk to another one of the exceptional young people who is riding on this bus with me as we tour North Dakota late at night. This is Jacy Greff. Jacy, what do you think about all of this?"

"This is the most fun I've ever had! I can't believe all the stuff that's happened today! I wish all this would never end!"

"Jacy, what would you like to tell all the people around the country who are watching right now?"

"I guess I'd just like to tell them that North Dakota is a great place to live and *please exercise!* It's really important!"

"Thanks, Jacy!" (He paused briefly.) "Has anyone ever told you that you're a very NICE young lady?!" (Jacy blushed.)

(Suddenly, there was a big commotion on the bus as everyone looked up in the sky!)

"Ladies and gentlemen, as I speak, it looks like four more helicopters are joining the other five helicopters already escorting The Starship Exercise. As I understand, there is an Air Force Base in Minot, and I would guess that these four helicopters are probably from that facility!

"I'm now joined by the Governor of North Dakota. Governor Ed, what do you think's going on?"

"I think everyone in North Dakota is having fun

with this! Obviously, the Minot Air Force Base was not about to be outdone by the Grand Forks Air Force Base!"

"Governor, do you expect any more surprises on this trip?"

"I wouldn't put anything past the people of this great state!"

"Well, Governor, we're going to have to return to our regularly scheduled program now, but we'll be back for another special report in half an hour. This is Tom Broklow reporting for NBC News on the road in North Dakota."

CHAPTER XXII

I had a feeling that no one in North Dakota slept that night. If people weren't actually part of the caravan in person, they were keeping track of its movement on the television and the radio.

It was close to one o'clock in the morning before we got to Williston, but the whole town seemed to be standing on the side of the road, screaming, yelling, waving, and singing *The Fitness Song*. A good share of the town got in their cars and trucks and joined our caravan.

After leaving Williston, Phil took this call from a Bismarck girl:

"Hi, I'm Becky Mueller from Bismarck, and I've got a question for Governor Ed."

Phil said, "Go ahead, Becky."

"Well, I'm a huge sports fan like you, Governor, and I was just wondering if there's one sports event that stands out in your mind as the most exciting ever?"

Governor Ed responded, "Hi, Becky! Yes, there is a sports moment that stands out in my mind as the most amazing I've ever seen, and it took place right there in Bismarck in1973! I was in the Civic Center watching the State Class A Boys Basketball Championsip Game between Minot and Fort Yates. Fort Yates was behind 8 points with 43 seconds to go in regulation. With almost no time remaining a Fort Yates player by the name of Wyman Archambault banked in a shot from the top of the key to put the game into a first overtime. To make a long story short, Fort Yates ended up winning that game in triple overtime, I think the score was 79-78 or something! It was unbelievable!"

Mark said, "I think Fort Yates had an outstanding player by the name of Eaglestaff on that team, too, didn't they, Governor Ed?"

"That's right, Mark," Governor Ed said. "If I remember right, Eaglestaff had 29 points in the game! Isn't it amazing that that game took place more than twenty years ago, and yet I'll bet anyone who was in the Civic Center that night remembers many details of what happened!"

"That is amazing!" Phil added.

The Starship Exercise Caravan headed south toward Beach, North Dakota. For the next three hours, we were driving through some of the most sparsely populated areas of the state. Still, even out in the middle of nowhere, people were standing on the side of the road, watching The Starship Exercise Caravan go by them. Several times, people on horses holding flashlights waved as we passed.

At Beach, we got back on Interstate 94, beginning the last stretch of our journey back to Bismarck. In the back of the bus, Prez continued to work contentedly on his new remote control unit. Chad and I went back to talk to him.

Chad asked, "Prez, is everything going all right?"

Prez had a very small screwdriver in one hand, and a partially assembled remote control unit on a box in front of him. "I think so," Prez replied. "I'm glad I've still got a few hours to go, though."

I told Prez, "I sure am glad I was part of this whole experience. You know, it's never boring hanging around you!"

"Well, thanks, Kevin. I have a feeling our excitement isn't over yet either."

"I sure hope not!" I exclaimed.

When we got to Medora, two of North Dakota's most famous and remarkable residents—Harold and Sheila Schafer—boarded our bus. They were not about to miss this historic event!

It was an incredible sight as the nine helicopters and The Exercise flew over The Painted Canyon area of the Badlands near Medora. The lights from those flying objects illuminated the Badlands just enough to provide a picture postcard image!

By the time we got to Dickinson, it was just light enough to see the Dakota Dinosaur Museum near the Interstate. Forty more miles down the road near Hebron we got another big surprise! The ladies of Hebron must have worked most of the night making caramel rolls to feed the whole caravan! As the caravan slowed to a snail's pace on Interstate 94, hundreds of Hebron's townspeople handed out the rolls and coffee!

"This is Phil Parker with Mark Armstrong reporting from the K-Fire Cruiser, now only about an hour outside of the Bismarck-Mandan area! I think that anyone who has had anything to do with this event the past 17 or so hours has to admit that there are really no words to describe how exciting and fun it has been!"

Mark said, "I wonder how many people in North Dakota got any sleep last night at all? I think this was an event no one wanted to miss any part of!"

Phil agreed, "No doubt about it! Well, let's get you caught up with the latest developments! We understand that even at this early hour of 6 a.m., thousands of people are lining the streets of Bismarck and Mandan, anticipating the arrival of The Starship Exercise Caravan!"

Mark continued, "We also have kept in contact with Prez all night and he has told us he hopes to have his new remote control ready before we get to Mandan so he can personally guide The Exercise as it flies over Mandan and Bismarck."

"Mark, this caravan has been a great experience for us, and also a great thing for our state! Thanks to Tom Broklow, the whole country has learned a lot about this great state of ours!"

"Yes, Phil, we should try to get Tom on the phone right now. Tom, do you have time to talk to us?"

"Hello, this is Tom. How are you guys feeling this morning?"

"Great!" Mark answered.

"A lot better after those caramel rolls back there in Hebron!" Phil said.

Tom said, "Only in your state would a whole caravan of cars be served fresh caramel rolls right on the Interstate!"

"Ya, Tom!" Mark said, with a laugh. "And, only in North Dakota would you actually *eat* caramel rolls given to you by complete strangers!"

Tom laughed and said, "I believe you're right,

Mark!"

Phil asked, "Tom, what are some of the impressions you're going to take away from this experience!"

"Of course, the sight of The Starship Exercise flying behind all of those helicopters in the dark of night is something I'll never forget! Also, the faces of all these great sixth graders who have ridden on this bus with your outstanding North Dakota Governor and all the rest of us! I feel really good inside to know that there are young people like this around! Also, I'll remember the faces of all of the people of your state who greeted us along the way!"

Mark said, "Tom, *you* will be one of the important parts of our memories of this experience! Thanks for being here with us!"

"I wouldn't have missed it for the world! I just hope the rest of the trip goes as smoothly as Prez wants it to!"

Phil said, "Thanks, Tom!"

CHAPTER XXIII

When we were ten miles outside of Mandan, Prez announced to everyone in the bus, "I think my remote control is ready!"

"Gee," Matt said with a playful smile, "you've got a whole *ten miles* to spare!"

"I just wanted to make things more exciting for all of us!" Prez declared.

Then, Prez said, "Could I ask everyone in the bus to do me a big favor? Before I try the new unit out, could we quickly pass it around to everyone on the bus for good luck?"

Chad said, "Prez, I didn't know you were superstitious."

"I just figure we can use all the help we can get," Prez replied.

As the remote control unit was being passed around, I glanced out the window at The Starship Exercise, now flying approximately a quarter of a mile ahead of us, at an altitude of about sixty feet. For just an instant, I wished

Prez's remote control unit wouldn't work, and we could continue following The Exercise wherever it would take us. Part of me didn't want this adventure to end.

When the remote control unit had been passed all around, Prez took it and walked to the front of the bus. "Here goes!" he said, as he turned the unit on. "Let's see if we can regain control of our starship!"

He began working the controls, but I couldn't see any change in the path of The Exercise. "What's happening?" Charles asked.

"It's not working!" Prez sounded a little desperate. "I thought I did everything right, but it's not responding!"

Governor Ed spoke anxiously, "Prez, we've only got three miles to the Sunset Exit into Mandan. What can we do?"

Suddenly, Jacy called from behind them, "**I'LL HIT IT!**"

Prez looked a little shocked! It was hard to imagine that Jacy had hit anyone or anything in her life! He turned around to face Jacy and asked, "What do you mean, **YOU'LL HIT IT**?! This is a delicate complex electronic device!"

"Just give it to me!" Jacy insisted. "I'll fix it!"

Everyone, including Prez, was stunned by Jacy's request. Prez finally *did* pass the remote control unit to Jacy!

Jacy delicately touched the entire surface of the remote

control with her hands, and then gave it a firm *slap* on the back with her right hand! After that, she passed the unit back to Prez and said, "Now try it."

Prez turned the unit on, worked the controls, and suddenly The Exercise started to slow down and lose altitude! "**IT WORKS! IT WORKS**!" Prez yelled with excitement.

Everyone in the bus celebrated! They hugged each other! They hugged Jacy! They cheered excitedly! **WE DID IT**! Prez had control of The Starship Exercise once again!

As soon as we exited Interstate 94 at the Sunset Drive Exit near Mandan, we became part of a huge celebration that my parents later said may have been bigger than the North Dakota Centennial Celebration in 1989! One thing that made our celebration so unique, though, was the fact that it took place a little past seven o'clock in the morning!

Everyone got an **AMAZING** show as the helicopters led The Starship Exercise overhead. Meanwhile, down below, a line of vehicles like no one had ever seen before was led through the streets by the six Highway Patrol cars *and* every police car and firetruck that the cities of Bismarck and Mandan could assemble!

The caravan worked its way down Mandan's Main Street, onto the Strip, over the Lewis and Clark Bridge, and finally to Prez's house on Pocatello Drive. All along the way, huge crowds cheered wildly, and held up signs and banners! This had to be the best early morning parade in history!

When we arrived at Prez's house, the helicopters headed for the Bismarck Airport. Meanwhile, Prez let The Starship Exercise fly in a large circular path over South Bismarck, as a huge crowd gathered in the neighborhood near Prez's house! Already waiting in Prez's front yard were Mayor Bob Dykshoorn of Mandan and Mayor Bill Sorensen of Bismarck, along with television crews from both KXMB and KFYR! They were part of a huge crowd that filled the whole neighborhood and spilled over into several other adjoining neighborhoods!

When we had all gotten out of the bus to join the mayors, Prez let The Exercise slowly circle one more time, then he guided it to a smooth landing right in front of us!

CHAPTER XXIV

The whole Starship Exercise experience started a fitness revolution in North Dakota! In the months that followed, the young people of our state kept the momentum going! In less than a year's time, our state had the fittest population in the country!

A survey taken in March showed that over eight-five percent of the people in North Dakota were exercising regularly! Meanwhile, The Starship Exercise became the symbol of the improved fitness and image of the state! People all over North Dakota were wearing Starship Exercise t-shirts with pride!

In April, the President of the United States took notice of our state's excellent fitness program! He announced that he was going to send a member of his National Committee on Physical Fitness to present a special award to the young people of the state for their efforts. Were we ever excited when we found out who the President was sending to Bismarck to present the award! It was Phil Jackson, coach of the Chicago Bulls!

My dad told me Phil Jackson was once a great basketball player at Williston High School and at the University of North Dakota. Later, he played for the New York Knicks of the NBA! I knew him as the super coach of the World Champion Chicago Bulls, my favorite professional basketball team!

The day before Phil Jackson was to arrive in Bismarck, Governor Ed called Dr. KK in the morning during math class. Dr. KK put the call on his speakerphone so we could all hear the conversation.

"Hi, Governor Ed! What's going on?"

"I was just wondering if your class could do me a big favor?" Governor Ed asked.

"You know we'll do anything for you, Governor Ed!" Dr. KK said.

"Well, I would like you and your class to meet Phil Jackson's private jet when it comes in tomorrow night! I told him about you and your class, and he wants to meet all of you!"

Our whole class cheered loudly when we heard this! When we had quieted down a little, Dr. KK said, "Did you hear our answer, Governor Ed?!"

"Yes, I did!" Governor Ed replied. "Would you mind if I picked you up at your school at six tomorrow night?"

"Bringing the bus again, Governor?" Dr. KK wondered.

"I thought it would bring back some good memories," the Governor replied.

"See you tomorrow, then, Governor Ed," Dr. KK said.

"**GOOD-BYE, GOVERNOR ED**!" we all yelled.

You should have heard the cheer that erupted when Dr. KK got off the phone!!

The next night, Governor Ed picked us up at Dorothy Moses School and we headed toward the Bismarck Airport! Everyone was really excited to have a chance to meet Phil Jackson's private jet!

When we got out to the airport, we watched the small jet land and taxi toward the terminal building. As it came to a stop, Governor Ed announced, "Oh, by the way, Phil told me he was bringing a friend along with him. His friend's a little shy, so he hopes we'll be extra nice."

At that time, Jessie Angell spotted two men getting off the jet, and she screamed, "Oh my gosh! **IT'S MICHAEL JORDAN**!!" Everyone looked out the window of the terminal, and couldn't believe it! It **WAS** Michael Jordan!

Prez said, "Governor Ed, do you mean *Michael Jordan* is Phil Jackson's shy friend?"

"Sorry, Prez, I had to make this a *little* surprising for all of you!"

That evening was one of the greatest times our class could have imagined! We all got to have dinner at the Governor's mansion with First Lady Nancy, Governor Ed, Phil Jackson, AND MICHAEL JORDAN!! **WHAT A DREAM COME TRUE!!**

Just before we had to leave that evening, Michael Jordan said, "Oh, I forgot to ask you. I've got tickets for all of you for our first playoff game in a couple of weeks against the Miami Heat! Anyone want to go?"

All of our eyes got huge, but everyone remained silent, as if in shock!

Governor Ed broke the brief silence when he said, "Before you answer, I'll take care of the transportation and hotel!"

"Are we taking the bus, Governor Ed?" Jacy wondered.

"No, I think we'll go by plane this time if it's all right with all of you!" Governor Ed replied.

"This is Chuck Bartholomay with Monica Hannan from KFYR-TV News in Bismarck. Today, the young people of North Dakota expected to receive a special award from a real North Dakota hero–Phil Jackson! But they got a real bonus along the way when Phil decided to bring his good friend along!"

Monica Hannan continued, "And we're not talking about just any friend, we're talking about the greatest basketball player of all time–Michael Jordan!"

"That's right, Monica! Michael Jordan spoke to over 60,000 of North Dakota's youth who had gathered on the lawn of the Capitol Mall here in Bismarck! Michael encouraged the youth of all ages in North Dakota to keep exercising and keep studying! Then Phil Jackson and Michael Jordan presented a special plaque from the President of the United States to Andrea Doerr, a Bismarck student who was chosen to represent all of the great youth of our state!"

"This is Tom Jensen with Bonnie Waldorf from KXMB-TV News in Bismarck. Today's visit by Michael Jordan and Phil Jackson was an appropriate finishing touch to an incredible school year for the youth of North Dakota! What better way for the people of North Dakota to celebrate being the fittest state in the Union!"

Bonnie continued, "Michael and Phil brought along five basketballs autographed by the entire Chicago Bulls Basketball Team. Governor Ed drew the names of the lucky winners from the youth gathered from all over the state! The winners were Jason Swanson from Grand Forks, Dan Weigel from Minot, Kari

Gillen from Fargo, Tiff Tello from Lisbon, and Kristy Kelsch from Hillsboro."

Tom Jensen concluded, "But I think all of us who were up at the Capitol today and all of the rest of us in the state of North Dakota should all feel like winners today! We truly are the GREATEST state in this GREAT country!"

ABOUT THE AUTHOR

Kevin Kremer was born and raised in Mandan, North Dakota, and has taught the past twenty-one years in Bismarck. He currently teaches fifth grade at Dorothy Moses Elementary School. Kevin's first book, *A Kremer Christmas Miracle*, was written as a Christmas present to his family, and was published in 1995. While writing that book, Kevin discovered how much fun it was to write about North Dakota people, places, and events. He truly believes that North Dakota is the greatest place in the world! He hopes The Pittsburgh Steelers win another Super Bowl before the beginning of the twenty-first century!

Sweetgrass Communications

For Additional Great Reading
By Kevin Kremer:

A Kremer
Christmas Miracle

KEVIN KREMER TITLES:

❏   0-9632837-4-X   Spaceship Over North Dakota $7.99
❏   0-9632837-2-3   A Kremer Christmas Miracle $6.99

Sweetgrass Communications, P.O. Box 3221, Bismarck, ND 58502

Please send me the books I have checked above. I am enclosing $_____
(please add $2.00 to cover shipping and handling). Send check or money
order — no cash or C.O.D.'s please.

Name _____

Address _____

City _____ State/Zip _____

Please allow four to six weeks for delivery. Offer good in the U.S.A. only.
Sorry, mail order not available to residents of Canada. Prices subject to change.